The Hag in the Woods

by

Deb Scudder

For Paul

Published in 2014 Copyright ©Deb Scudder
All rights reserved.

The village of Annisthorpe and all characters in this novel are fictional. Any resemblance to real persons, living or dead, is purely coincidental.

Chapter One

I don't do it, of course. That would be suicide. I don't tell them to stop, leave her alone. I don't even slow down as I walk past, eyes to the ground, glancing up now and then to check they haven't noticed me. Her eyes peep out between their blazered shoulders, seeking an escape, but she doesn't look at me, thank goodness. I think about saying something, providing a distraction so she can get away, but I know how hard it is to move under the weight of so much unwarranted vitriol and spite. She might not be able to take advantage of it if I did shout out 'Oi, stop it!' or 'Get off her!' or any of the other pathetic utterances in my head. I feel tiny, my neck burning, the heat prickling up to my ears. I keep walking. The dust from the gravel greys my shoes. I'm an idiot.

She'll be all right. They don't do anything physical, those boys. It's all words and bile. I should know. I kick gravel up with each step, imagining kicking it onto their shoes instead, or into their eyes. I keep my eyes down, seeing nothing but the endless grey crags and their dust, and the toe of my shoe pushing forwards, and receding back, the other one forwards, receding. I'm approaching the classroom, the gravel stones packing closer together as more feet have weighed them down. I get there far sooner than seems reasonable. The redness must have gone down, but I rub my neck under my right ear to try and erase the last of it anyway. I look down for one last second before I have to go in. I need more time to gather myself, to grow tall again after the humiliation of wanting to help the girl, but being too useless. So many times I've been desperate for help myself and none came, and then someone else needs it and I do nothing. She is probably still back there (I'm not going to look behind to see) surrounded by boys taller than her, being made late for lessons. I can't look anyone in the eye as I enter the classroom.

These classrooms are along one edge of the playing field. They were supposed to be temporary while they extended the main building, but have been here for twenty years now, the teacher said. The first time I saw them, when I started comprehensive three years ago, I thought they looked exotic, like Gypsy caravans. They're nothing like that, but I prefer them to normal classrooms. I like the way the floor bounces and creaks when you walk across it, and there's a feeling of being outdoors, which we are I suppose, like going caravanning.

Another good thing about them is if you have a teacher who doesn't pounce on you the minute your eyes drift to look out of the window, there is quite a nice view. Well, a green one, anyway, of the field with its fading white lines on the grass and distant goal posts. It's better than the grey and brown one of the car park, or the windows of other classrooms across a dreary courtyard with nothing growing in it except a few strangled dandelions stretching their necks out, yearning for a light source.

I've never said anything to those boys, either to

provoke them or in defence of myself or anyone else. Even if asked a direct question I've never answered them. I mean, what are you supposed to say to 'What are you looking at?' when you didn't even notice they were there? I'm looking at the clouds above the roof of this stinking school, don't you think they look like heaps of mashed potato? Or, 'Who do you think you are?' Well, since you ask, I'm Tom, nice to make your acquaintance. Maybe that's why they pick on me, because I don't say anything. You'd think they'd get bored.

I saw the girl at lunchtime and she looked okay, chatting with her friends. My relief at this is tempered with a hammering shame that I didn't do anything to help her this morning, but I never have the right words, or the gumption.

*

I'm walking along the main road, glad that another school day is over. My head is down and I drag my feet along with each step, trying to close my ears to the clattering noise of the traffic. I despise the concrete and the cars. Any time I see a shepherd's purse or some other forlorn plant forcing its way through the cement I rejoice inside. It cheers me to see a triumph of nature over man, no matter how small. Whenever I can, I walk on the grass verge instead of the tarmac. It's more comfortable; not so hard on my feet.

Glancing up as I reach the junction where I must cross the road, I see a dark spot, out of place. Across the road, laid flat along the path, is the unmistakable shadow of a cat, but it's all wrong. It lays diagonally, and looks painted on, too. It's too dark, somehow. I look around in case anyone else has seen it too, but the other children swarming away from the school are too preoccupied with their own thoughts and conversations to notice it. When I turn back it's gone. I search along the path in both directions, but there is no sign of a retreating cat, and anyway the shadow was too big to be cast by a real cat. It's mid-afternoon on a grey day with no sun. The street lights won't come on for hours.

I think about the cat for the rest of the walk home, until I'm swallowed up in the warmth and comfort there so that thoughts of the shadow slip away and I forget.

We're having dinner on our laps as it's fish and chips

from the chip shop, a special treat, and we haven't bothered with plates. We eat it with the little wooden forks from the chippy, as though we're enjoying a day out at the seaside instead of all huddled inside the house.

'The Old Wood is up for sale, Tom, did you know?' Helen says. 'Probably be bought by some developer. We'll have those awful new-build houses to look at before long, I should think, instead of lovely old trees.' Her voice cracks. 'That wood's been there since anyone can remember. Some of those trees are hundreds of years old. Do you remember that big old beech tree that used to be there?'

'No.'

'It was such a beauty. Shame that lightning got it that time. I was really hoping they wouldn't have to cut it down, but it wasn't safe, they said.'

I'm gazing at the television screen, but not watching it. 'I can't stand the thought of them building houses where those trees are, Helen,' I mutter around a mouthful of fish. 'I hope no-one buys it. Or if they do, I hope they buy it to look after the trees and make sure no-one harms them.'

The thought of someone from outside the village buying the Old Wood, chopping all the trees down and replacing them with a bunch of poxy houses makes me feel sick. The word 'poxy' is huge in my mind. It's one of my favourites. I saw a documentary on punk by accident, and one of the people on that kept using it. It's perfect; not actually a swear word, but holding enough venom to be massively satisfying to say. I wouldn't dare to say it in front of my grandparents though. They would probably think it is a swear word and I don't want to offend them. Poxy new-build houses.

I finish my mouthful and gulp in a deep breath. That's something my gran's taught me for times like this. 'Deep breaths, Tom,' she would soothe, doing it with me. 'In,' she'd take a big breath and hold her mouth shut as if she were underwater, 'and out,' she would blow the air out again. We did it together until I was calm. I don't need her to do it with me these days. I do it on my own, although I can see her looking at me, her lips moving as though she is doing it too, willing me to calm my breathing.

When I lie down that night I keep my arms out over the top of the duvet and press my hands together under my chin, as if in prayer. It feels stupid, but I do it anyway. My lips move but no sound comes out, as I ask whatever deity might be listening to make sure the trees are not cut down to build houses, or anything else, please.

Chapter Two

I live with my grandparents, Helen and Bob. There was a car accident when I was six - I wasn't in the car, I was staying with Helen and Bob - and my mum and dad both died. They were going to view a new house in the next village but came off the road; one of those long, straight roads Lincolnshire has, with the occasional right angle bend tossed in every few miles to break the monotony. It was winter and there was black ice. My mum died straight away, right there in that ditch. My dad, who was driving, endured for a few days in hospital - he never knew anything about it - before dying too. I simply stayed here instead of going home.

That's how I came to live in Annisthorpe, instead of where we were before. We're way down in the south of Lincolnshire, close to the border with Leicestershire. It's called the Vales of the county, or so I've read. I've never heard anyone actually call it that, though. We're only about ten miles from where I was born, but I've never been back there as far as I can remember, and it feels as remote now as if it were up there on Skylab, studying the sun. The landscape around Annisthorpe is broad and open, falling and swaying like the tide coming in on the coast, so far away, and there are not many people living in it.

The next day at school news of the sale of the Old Wood hangs in the air like a threat. A property developer company from down south is already showing interest, according to particles of conversations I overhear. It's thought that they will buy the land for new houses. My stomach flips when I hear that, but there's a part of me hoping they're wrong and it's nothing but rumours. It even gets a mention in assembly, the headmaster intoning in that dull way of his that it would be a great loss to the village. For once, I agree with him. It's a few days later when the news comes in from more official channels; the building company from London has bought the Old Wood.

*

In my dream there are shadows everywhere. They

plaster themselves to every surface, growing and changing, shrinking again. I am in the woods, the trees black against the sky. At first I thought the smell was burnt toast, but it's the tang from a bonfire somewhere in the village.

The shadows are all around me, and my belly tingles, as though I'm excited about something. I am inert. If I did move, it could be nothing compared to the constant waves of shadows morphing all around me. Their spirits lean in and out, grow tall and short, like flames licking out from that bonfire I can smell. Sometimes they are animal-shaped; foxes, wolves, dogs, and then smaller animals, a stoat and then a rabbit, then a mole, a shrew. At other times they appear humanoid, from tiny pixie-like beings to giants.

They dance around me in the woods all night like a dark kaleidoscope, until I wake at two in the morning and look at the ceiling for a long time.

The street light at the far end of the front garden provides enough light for me to see. I'm used to it by now, but when I first moved here I struggled to sleep for weeks, because it is at exactly the wrong angle to where I want my bed. My bed has to be where it is, that's non-negotiable. It has to be under the window. But the light from the street lamp softened over the months as I got used to it, and now on the rare occasions I have to sleep somewhere other than my bedroom at home, I miss it. There is something reassuring about its steady presence through the night. It knows exactly when to come on, and when to go off without me doing a thing.

I can't close my eyes. I sense the shadows in my dream were only for me. They have a message, or something they need from me, I don't know which. Eyes steady on the yellow glow from the street light on the ceiling, I let out a short laugh at how ludicrous that sounds. Just a dream, Tom, that's all it was.

I feel a pulling sensation, like a tug in the direction of the Old Wood. Not many people go there anymore, and I'm not sure if I ever have. I walk past it - everyone does, there is a busy road running adjacent to it - but I don't recall ever going in. I resist the urge to get up and sneak out of the house for a clandestine visit there.

Comfortable on my back, hands folded on my chest, I gaze through half-closed eyes at the light on the ceiling. After a time my eyes shut and I sleep.

June, 1976

The sickly red carpet in the hallway. I like to vroom my Matchbox cars up and down the curving lines in its garish golden patterns. Up and down, around this leafy part, over the top of those two petals, back down the stem of this twisty Triffid sprouting in the pile.

My mum's voice comes down the stairs. I smell her perfume before I see her, heavy and floral. She's patting her hair, reeking of hairspray, and fussing with the neck tie on her blouse, trying to get it straight. She stops in front of the mirror by the front door to examine herself. Such a pretty mum.

'Shall I change this top, Terry?' she calls up the stairs to my dad. Vowels drift down from the bedroom but I can't make out what he says and neither can Mum. She tuts and goes back upstairs. I go back to my vrooming. Vroooooom. Vrooooooom.

I don't like it when they go out. I like my evenings to be settled; bit of telly, nice warm bath, bedtime stories, snuggles. I get those at Grandma's too, but it's not the same. She doesn't sit the same way as Mum when she's reading the stories, and her voice isn't right. The bath is always too cold, the food not as interesting. Grandma's hair is curly like Mum's, and like mine. We're a curly haired family. The little man I imagine driving the car I'm holding has curly hair too. He's a hero. He goes around in his car rescuing people, and sorting them out when they're in trouble.

Dad's hair isn't curly, it's wavy. He's always very keen to make the distinction. I don't know why. Looks curly to me. He's coming down the stairs, making them creak. He's heavier than Mum, harder to push over when you're play-fighting. He's like a boulder, doesn't move at all even though I push with all my strength. Doesn't move at all. It's amazing. I don't like that. I'd like him to pretend and move a little bit so I wouldn't feel so tiny and helpless. But he doesn't move, ever.

'Come on Tommy, put your cars away. We have to be off in a minute.'

I look up at him, way, way up there near the ceiling

light. Look how high! 'Okay,' I say, and scoop my cars up, pushing them towards the box in the corner they all came out of, chucking them in so they crash into each other.

I have my slippers on. I can keep them on to go to Grandma's, she doesn't mind. They're tartan like my dad's. I wanted some just like his, and that's what I got. They're brilliant. I like to put my finger under the little elastic patches on either side that stretch so you can get your foot in, and slide it around, watching the bump moving. Mum says I moved like that when I was inside her tummy, but I don't believe her. I was never inside her tummy. I wouldn't be able to fit or breathe.

Mum is coming back downstairs, the scent of her perfume too strong, and tragic because it means she's leaving me. She never wears perfume when she's staying at home and baking fairy cakes with me, or when we're cuddled up on the sofa with Morecambe and Wise on. She only wears it when she's leaving, but she does always come back! Her top is different. It was white before, now it's red and she has no neck tie to worry about. She's glowing, coming past me in her chunky-heeled sandals. I watch her toes go past, encased in American Tan tights, caught in a net like fish in the sea. They're both in the kitchen, so I think I'd better join them or they might go without me.

We always use the back door. The front door only opens for the postman and other delivery people who don't know that we only use the back door. The back door is nearer to the car, so it makes sense. The garage is behind the house, the other side of the back garden.

Mum catches me up in her arms, so I get an extra big lungful of the floweriness of her, and can see her face close up. Shiny mouth, powdery eyes. So beautiful, like a painting!

We're outside. It's still light and the hedge is full of birds chittering at each other. I really want to know what they're saying. I ask Mum, but she doesn't know. Dad is getting the car out of the garage, a much bigger version of one of my Matchbox cars, and I realise I've forgotten teddy. I start to cry. There's a fullness in my chest that I can't speak around. Teddy! We go back into the house, as Mum is super-clever and has worked out that teddy is missing. She leaves me standing in the kitchen, whimpering, while she runs upstairs to get him.

We are in the car. I lie across the back seat

pretending to be on a chaise longue in a luxurious moving living room. I watch the heads of the street lights, not on yet, go past. It looks like the same one going round and round, not different ones all in a row. Mum and Dad are talking about Brenda and Robert, who they are going to have dinner with. Brenda is pregnant again, Robert's been promoted. 'It's so exciting!' Mum says. I close my eyes and squeeze teddy.

Chapter Three

It's funny, as I'm so interested in local folk tales, that I've never delved much into the most obvious one. The tale of The Hag in the Woods is the first of these kinds of stories I remember Helen telling me. She and Bob have a great enthusiasm for folklore, and have a shelf on the bookcase in the hall dedicated to the subject. I like the books on that shelf, but I love to hear the stories more. When Helen recites one of her favourite tales it's like a gift to me. In The Hag in the Woods the action takes place right here in Annisthorpe, in the Old Wood. Such is its all-pervading, this-is-just-how-it-is nature, I've never felt the need to look any further into it, until now. The story is so deeply entrenched in one place, and that place is so much a permanent and ancient part of the place I live in, that the presence of it is as natural as the presence of the trees, or the cave-like feature at one end of the wood, where the ground grows swampy and uncertain. The fact of the story is as obvious to me as the fact that those trees lose their leaves each autumn, and grow new ones every spring.

My grandparents tell me other stories that are supposed to have happened around this area, and many from further afield too. There are tales of grim little people who tie your shoelaces together if you stand still for too long, their tiny giggles just audible as you fall to your knees when you try to walk. There are tales of more prepossessing creatures who lure people with promises of secrets revealed and eternal happiness to the marshy edge of the forest and, through sheer force of numbers, hold their heads face down in the shallow water of the long grasses there, ensuring their mouths and noses stay in the peaty wetness until they drown.

Sometimes I read that these little people are real and not imagined; that they are a remnant from a time, thousands upon thousands of years ago, when their kind inhabited these parts. They are elves or sprites, pixies or gnomes or hobgoblins who have not gone, but have remained, when all of their kin were driven to languish forever inside the hills. They continue to live here in this implausible pocket of reality as though nothing happened. I have looked into these and other tales, but they do not have the gravity, nor the immediacy, of the tale of the Hag.

The tale of the Hag is one of those primal stories that speaks to the core of the nature of human children, moss, and deep, dark places we do not like to probe too much. One of those things you don't look at too closely for fear of uncovering something you will regret seeing. And now the exact same trees that feature in that story are under direct threat from people from elsewhere who cannot possibly understand their importance, and who only want to make money.

There are other shadows now, always incongruous and intriguing. I've come to expect to see them, and look out of the corners of my eyes when out and about to try and catch them. They're easier to see that way; if you look straight at them they become opaque, camouflaging themselves.

I try to put thoughts of them aside, however, as I leave the haven of my room with its squishy bed and its posters; Depeche Mode, The Human League and a small one on the wall over the chest of drawers of

Bananarama that I ripped out of Smash Hits. I also have a small black and white portable television and even my own video player, splayed out on the floor. There's no space for them anywhere else. I have all three Star Wars films, and some old classics with people like James Dean and Marlon Brando in them. I'll watch anything, it's the stories I like, and the screen fascinates me; all the mesmerising shades of grey between black and white, and the music. Sometimes I put a film on not to watch it, but to have the music on in the background while I'm writing, or dozing. It helps me to relax, and drowns out the voices of the kids at school in my head, always taunting.

Downstairs, I find Grandma sitting next to Bob on the sofa, enjoying the latest Crossroads. I sit in the armchair by the standard lamp and wait for the programme to finish, enduring what feels like an eternity of terrible acting, followed by the dirge of a theme tune.

I switch the lamp on after Bob turns the television off, missing its light, and ask Helen if she would tell me the story of the Hag in the Woods again. Bob disappears with a wave of the newspaper. He'll be in the kitchen if anybody needs him.

'You haven't heard that one from me for years, Tom!' Helen says, unable to keep the surprise out of her voice.

I suppose I am getting a little old for these stories. She must have assumed I wouldn't be asking for them anymore, as it's been so long. She twists herself around on the sofa to face me, hitching one leg bent up underneath her, the other foot resting on the floor.

Helen is a petite woman, with an inquisitive, delicate face, and nearly always smiling. Her hair is starting to show white strands and frizzes out from her head, preferring to grow outwards into the world, rather than merely obey gravity and hang like most people's hair does. It's curly, but if she gets caught in the rain it becomes one fuzzy mass, like the hair on one of my old Action Man dolls.

She loves reading stories almost as much as she loves telling them to other people, and clearly relishes this chance to tell her favourite again. She settles her hands down to rest on the sofa beside her.

'A long time ago, in the Old Wood of Annisthorpe, there lived a terrible old hag. If you lived there at the time you would have known all about her. Your parents would have given dire warnings again and again that you should not play in the part of the wood where the Hag lived, that you should stay away, because to venture into the territory of the Hag was to certainly die.'

Helen's eyes glimmer in the lamp light, but she's still smiling.

'The parents of the village told their children that the Hag was blue all over, from the roots of her lank, thinning hair to the nails on her scaly old toes. Her skin had a sort of luminescence about it, so that you could see her even in the dark, looming like some slow, lumbering ghost out of that cave she lived in.

'She was so old she was bent almost double, but had no stick to help her walk. She stumbled about on her bare blue feet, back bent at almost ninety degrees, with her head permanently cocked up and listening, like a blackbird listens for worms underground. She was listening for children nearby.

'Her hair was as grey as a thundercloud and laid itself in a slick of grease down her back, plastering to her sloping shoulders. The skin of her calves, feet, arms and face was all exposed and so saggy and stretched by time and gravity that she barely looked human. Maybe she wasn't.

'Her eyes were black and drooping, always encrusted with globs of sticky green stuff, always running. They were sharp as pins, mind, those eyes. Never missed a thing.

'Such lips as she may once have had were now receded to such an extent that her mouth looked less like a mouth and more like a hole torn into the loose fabric of her face by a barbed hook. The wrinkles that beset her entire being multiplied here around that unfriendly hole, creating the impression that they were all escaping there, rushing into the black toothless pit beyond. Not quite toothless, though; she possessed one, hanging like a stalactite from the front of her top gum. That solitary tooth would have overhung her bottom lip if she had one, being over an inch long and as yellow and toxic as one of those exotic frogs you've seen pictures of. Just as slimy, too.'

I don't remember half of these details from previous tellings of the story. I think she is beefing it up as I'm older now, adding things more likely to scare a fourteen year old, but I don't mind.

I ease myself down further into the armchair, getting comfortable. Helen is not the only one enjoying herself. If she carries on like this, I might be able to forget about school and the niggling worry about the shadows, which keeps popping up despite my efforts to push it down.

As Grandma pauses to adjust her glasses and wipe her nose on a handkerchief she's found tucked in the sleeve of her jumper, the seed of an idea forms in my mind. I would like to film this story, out in the Old Wood before it's destroyed. My eyes drift from Helen, who is secreting the handkerchief back in her jumper, as I imagine where to get a camera from, the angles I'll use to film the story, how I can evoke the right atmosphere... I blink and look back to my grandma, who is drawing breath, ready to continue the story, still sitting in that awkward looking way of hers (she swears it's comfortable). The ends of her hair flicker and tremble as she gives her head a quick shake.

'But if you think all that was bad enough...' I remember what's coming and allow myself a smile, '... you just wait until you hear about her dress!' She pauses, moving her eyes from side to side, hands spread flat over thin air to indicate the level of tension here. I laugh out loud, and Helen winks at me.

'The dress the old Hag wore, all the time, never changing, was made entirely from the skins of children who had ventured too far in the forest. She would rip their skins off, none too carefully, using nothing but her hands, for she had no truck with man-made tools. She would stitch them together with threads made from her own hair, or sometimes the child's hair if it was long enough, feeding them through holes made by her longest fingernail. It was five inches long, that nail, and as bent and gnarled as the rest of her, yellow-green and springing from her left little finger. It was stronger than bones, that nail, stronger than iron, and ended in a point as savage as any wolf's fang.

'So, she fashioned her dress, tailor-made to fit her lumpy, misshapen body. Her own sordid version of Haute Couture, if you please.'

Helen wrinkles her nose at the thought of it, and I mirror her expression.

'She captured the children like this...' I beam at her, moving closer for the next bit, plonking myself next to her on the sofa. I want to be inside the story, with no distinction between it and the real world. I want the story to be the real world, if only for a few minutes.

'In front of the cave in which the old Hag lived there grew a huge beech tree. It took a grown man ten paces to walk around its trunk, and its branches formed a protective canopy over the forest. In the autumn children could bury themselves neck deep in the beech nuts and leaves that the tree dropped. And of course, climbing to the top of the giant beech became a favourite challenge among the children, young and old alike, who would shout and whoop, egging each other on to go one branch higher. One more, go on!

'The Hag's bower was well hidden behind a rise in the land there, and not usually noticed by anyone except children who got particularly high in the tree, or anyone foolish enough to wander over the ridge to stand exposed on her horizon. If people did spot the cave they usually didn't give it much thought, or bother to investigate. It wasn't even a proper cave, just a hollow under some ancient tree roots that looked uninhabited.

'Anyway, where that tree happened to grow made it all the easier for the Hag in the cave to attempt to garner more fabric so that perhaps she could have another dress to wear sometimes.' I am listening, but my thoughts keep drifting back to my film idea. Maybe I will do it. Find a camera somehow, or borrow one, and make a film in the Old Wood. I bring my full attention back to Helen.

'The way she caught the children was like this: if a child ended up on that ridge, silhouetted against the trees like a trophy on a mantelpiece, or if they climbed high enough in the tree to be able to see her in her bower, she had the power to make the wind change and freeze them where they were. They would rock, suspended, still conscious and aware, but utterly unable to move or make a sound. If they were up in the tree they would topple, frozen in the same shape they had when the wind changed, and fall through the branches, knocking this way and that, until they landed with a thump among the beech nuts and debris at the bottom. The old Hag would then drag herself across to them. She would poke her black little tongue out of the corner of her mouth in concentration as she scraped her feet across the ground, her hair swinging lazily.

'When she got to the child, it was not too much effort for her to grab their hair or jacket and drag them back to the cave over the bumpy ground. She was stronger than she looked, that old crone. She took them into the deepest part of the cave, where all the bones of her previous victims were piled. In that damp earth, she began her feast. First were the eyes - they were her favourite part. She popped them out and sucked them into her mouth, cackling at the way they burst and all the eyeball juices ran down her throat. Yum!

'She liked her meat fresh, and would not touch it once it was more than a day old, so she gorged herself on each fresh child she caught, sitting in her dank underworld moistly chewing with her hardened gums (as good for chewing as any teeth) on muscle and sinew until there were nothing but bones left. Hand over hand, the bits of the child went into that hole, and were masticated for the longest time, before disappearing down her gullet where the acids and toxins of her foul intestines finished the job off. Children were all she ate, and she could go a long time between feasts, so when she caught a fresh rosy-cheeked child, who only moments before had been running and laughing, heart pumping, breath pluming in and out, she was the happiest Hag in the world.

'And that, Thomas, is why the parents of Annisthorpe are always warning their children not to go into the Old Wood, for fear that the Hag will espy them and have another feast.' Helen finishes, triumphant, a satisfied smile on her lips.

'Is it real, Gran?'

'I'm not sure, Tom, but it's been real enough to scare small children for a long time since before I can remember. Real enough for that, definitely.'

We look at each other for a long time. Helen is one of those rare people who emanate kindness. It's there in her eyes and the curve of her mouth. I'm daydreaming about my film when she interrupts my thoughts.

'How's school?'

'Hmm,' I wish she hadn't changed the subject. 'Same as always, Gran.' I pull a face to suggest that school is neither here nor there and I don't want to talk about it. Helen shifts her legs - they get stiff after a while of sitting like that - and stretches out, propping her feet up on the coffee table, her tartan slippers perched on a magazine. She gives me her knowing look.

'Out with it then. What are you thinking?'

It's useless to pretend I wasn't thinking anything. 'Do

you know anyone with a video camera?'

She thinks for a moment. 'I don't think so, no. What have you got in mind?'

'I want to film something in the Old Wood, before they chop it all down,' I gulp, taken by surprise at the thought of all those beautiful trees lying on the ground, cleared for building. I might cry. Money-grabbing bastards. I learnt that word last week from the other children at school, and I like it very much. It feels so good to say. Bastards! I feel a little better already, and the word is only in my mind.

'Hmm, maybe try that second-hand place in town. I can lend you the money if you like, if you haven't got enough from your pocket money? You'll have to be quick if you want to do that though. I heard the deal was all done now and they're on their way with the bulldozers.' Even Gran can't keep the vitriol out of her voice when she talks about the developers. The Old Wood is special to the people of the village, even if they no longer go there.

Chapter Four

Helen's face is serene, looking out of the bus window at the passing houses and people. Bob refuses to drive into town on a Saturday; parking is a nightmare, he says. We are in search of a video camera and some blank tapes. Helen is a great people-watcher, and I can see her indulging now. She can sit for an hour at least in the High Street of the town, doing nothing except watch the world go by. That might be where I get it from, because I'm like that too. Daydreamers, Bob calls us, but then follows it up with, 'Life would be very boring, though, without you two,' and a twinkly smile.

The charity shop hasn't got any video cameras, only some old still ones. One is called a Brownie, with the viewfinder on the top instead of at the back. I peer through, seeing my grandparents and the shop shelves through a blotchy convex screen, tinted with sepia. I vow to get one sometime to try it out. There's a Kodak Instamatic too, so pleasing to hold. Neat, compact, tactile, and with the added bonus it will slot into my jacket pocket. I plan to get one of those, too. I think of having it sitting in my pocket when I'm out and about, and I can simply slip it out and start snapping, enjoying the rounded corners of its casing, the rough texture on the back pressing against my nose as I look through the viewfinder.

We leave the charity shop empty-handed, and wander down the High Street, chatting and looking in shop windows. We come upon a small electrical shop. It's one of those old independent shops that seems to have been there forever, that are such a fixture on the street they become invisible. We had all forgotten about it. In the window is a second hand video camera. I stop walking the instant I see it, staring in disbelief. I'd given up on finding anything, but there, right in front of me, is a video camera just like the one I've been holding in my head since listening to Gran's story.

Helen laughs at the look on my face as I gawp at it.

'Tom, you can have it if you like! Look, it's only £50. You have most of that saved up, and your granddad and

I can put the rest in.' She reaches up to put her arm around my shoulders, making me feel small even though I'm inches taller than her.

Sometimes I feel so grown up, and then other times, like now, I'm a small boy again. I look at her with a big daft grin. I simply can't believe it. I beam at Helen and Bob, and start to laugh, the excitement bubbling up and infecting my shoulders, making them rattle up and down.

I clap my hands together and stride into the shop, overcome with a rare confidence. Everything is falling into place. As soon as I'm inside, however, in the dark enclosed space of the shop, I realise what I'm doing and shrink back by the door to let Helen and Bob go through so they can do the talking. I'm sheepish under the scrutiny of the shopkeeper, standing with his hands spread out on the counter.

He opens his mouth to speak to me but I take a step back, avoiding eye contact, indicating that he should talk to the grown ups. I hover between Helen and Bob as they chat to him. He's pleased to see us, things have been quiet lately in the old independent electrical shop, even on Saturdays.

We leave the shop with the video camera and some tapes for it in a stiff green canvas bag, which I hug to myself all the way home. It's one of the more modern types of camera that you rest on one shoulder while filming. Not too big, but big enough to be 'proper' in my mind. I am ecstatic with it, and never want to put it down.

That night, as I snuggle down in bed with the video camera placed carefully on the floor by my side - I don't want to let it get too far away in case it turns out to be not real after all - I reflect on the day, running it in my mind, like a tape.

Shadows.

I hadn't noticed at the time. By the little electrical shop we got the camera from, there were shadows.

I saw them in the same instant that I saw the camera, yet the camera was all that registered in my mind. They are in the corners of my eyes where they always are, left and right, small animal-looking shadows coming towards me. By the time I move closer to the shop, they're not there anymore, and there aren't any real animals about to cast those shadows. I would have noticed that.

I nuzzle down further under my duvet, making the dark stripes on the cover crinkle up under my chin, and look at the light across the ceiling coming from the street lamp outside.

I let my eyes go out of focus and try to concentrate, running the tape of the afternoon again in my head. I thought the shadows were moving, but it wasn't that. They weren't moving in the sense of walking along or running, they were growing, as though the light behind which created them was receding, or the sun was sinking in the sky. They appeared and grew longer, trying to reach me, and then vanished.

Blinking with heavy eyelids, I turn to lie on my side facing the window. I like to have the curtains open a little so I can look out at the sky. Tomorrow I will ask Bob and Helen if they saw anything.

They didn't, of course. I already knew that somewhere in the base of my stomach before I asked and immediately felt an idiot for raising the subject. Helen gave me a quizzical look, and Bob wore his usual resigned but happy expression, as though he lives in a house full of mad people, but quite enjoys it.

I'm going to the Old Wood with my camera this

weekend, but the shadows are making me uneasy. They are around more of the time, in a greater variety of places, and it is increasingly apparent that they are only here for me. They play on my mind most of the time I'm awake, and they have parts in my dreams, too, if only in supporting roles.

I daren't bring the subject up at school. I'm already the butt of everybody else's jokes. Starting to talk about animal shadows that occur when there is no light and no animals, and that apparently only I can see, would only make things worse. There is not one person I can confide in. No special teacher who would understand, and certainly not any of the other pupils. The one or two who are brave enough to be seen hanging around with me occasionally cannot be trusted with this. It would alienate them, and probably ensure that they never spoke to me again.

I go through the days until the weekend, on the surface performing all the social functions required of me, but underneath brooding as I see the shadows more often.

There is no ill feeling coming from them, I don't think they're malignant, they are merely there. I've come to expect to see them every day, and if they don't show up I fall to thinking about where they might be instead, and why they have snubbed me.

Getting to know my new camera is going well. It's a simple device and I've already done a couple of short practice films around the house, capturing Helen making marmalade and creating a rancid orange fug that fills the whole house, and Bob in the garden training his peas to grow up the stakes he provides for them.

The images the camera produces are far crisper than I expected from an old second hand model, which makes me think it must hardly have been used before, maybe bought by someone in a rush of enthusiasm and then abandoned in the attic or shed for years before the clear-out that landed it in the electrical shop. That's not going to happen with me. I'm going to get my money's worth out of this lovely old machine. I've got a list in my room of all the ideas for films I'm going to make, fuelled by my dreams and all the tales I've heard dozens of times. First on the list is the Old Wood.

*

Shadows are all around the house these days, inside

and out, all the time, constantly shifting, growing and shrinking, but never leaving. There are more in the house and garden than anywhere else I go. Sometimes I see one on my way to or from school, but never in the school itself. If I pop to the shop or the park, I can expect to see one or two lurking at the edge of the path or low down on a garden wall. But the house is full of them. They've found hiding places, under the side board, under the coffee table, behind the television. I'm sure there must be one or two under my bed, although I don't look. There is always one in my wardrobe when I go in to get fresh clothes, one behind the curtains when I open them in the mornings, and one in the tiny bin in the bathroom.

The shadows are rooted to their spots, they don't move around the house. They stay in the particular place they've chosen, and grow or shrink, tilt left or right, from their bases, as though a lamp is being moved around to make them dance. They move both while I'm looking at them and when I try to ignore them. I often turn away and back again to find the shadow now at a different angle, or two feet taller than it was before.

On Friday night my room is full of them. They know

something, and it is to do with my visit to the woods tomorrow, I'm sure. There are so many more of them, now, and they are keeping me company in a way that not many humans have ever done. These days, they're as constant as the light on my ceiling from the street lamp all night, and if they went away, I would miss them.

I wriggle under my duvet, getting into the best position on my back for observing the light on the ceiling and the column of sky outside I can see through the gap in the curtains, my head propped at the perfect angle on the pillows. My eyes go out of focus as I let my imagination wander. I do this most nights and have noticed that the shadows grow in response. There is something familiar about them, like the trees in the wood surrounding anyone who walks there. Trees move and shift too, but are not scary.

The room away from the light on the ceiling grows a shade darker as the shadows creep up the walls, leaving their posts for the first time (that I've noticed) and moving onto the ceiling. They swarm to that stripe of light, dimpled by the textured paintwork Bob put there to cover the cracks, but do not encroach into it. They realise it's my light, and are respecting that. I have wild thoughts when I get my mind into this state. It's best at Christmas when I sit in front of the tree and unfocus my eyes until all the different coloured lights blur, first becoming stars and then supernovas, all merging into one another. The tree looks best like that.

For a long time I think about school and the people there, young and old. I see their faces and hear their words in a faint, detached way, like a dream. I'm wallowing in one of my favourite reveries. I have been in an accident, or am suffering from some serious illness or other, and am in hospital. A large group of pupils from school get together to make a huge get well card, and collect money to buy me chocolates. They come to see me and crowd round the bed, every one of them keen to see me and to say kind things to me. They come every day. The card wobbles on the little bedside cabinet under the weight of itself. It's bright pink with tissue paper pictures stuck on. I can't make out what the pictures are meant to be, but it's bright and cheering. Even though I'm in the hospital, I'm so happy that they care after all. For so long I wanted someone, anyone, to give a monkey's about me, and here they all are. They liked me all along. What happened at school was an act. The hospital is warm and my friends (the word is alien in my mind) smile and chat with me and include me in their jokes. I feel such a warm glow and at the same time such sorrow that I have to make myself stop thinking about it. I blink my eyes back into focus before any tears can fall.

At some point while I'm thinking about the hospital, the shadows stop moving and form into one mass stretching across the ceiling and down the walls, leaving a space for the strip of light from outside.

I hug the duvet to myself and look through the gap in the curtains, a tiny smile making the corner of my mouth twitch. I'm looking forward to tomorrow. The video camera is all set up with a fresh tape in place, batteries on full power. I have little idea what I will capture, but in a way that's not the point. I'm excited to get out there and see those trees, and film them before they disappear for good. My eyes drift as I try to trace the stars of Orion, barely visible against the glare of the street light. With one last glance up to the ceiling to note the shadows are still one indistinct block, making the room a tad darker than it was previously, I close my eyes.

In my dream the shadows recede, crawling back down the walls and gathering together by the door of my bedroom, smaller and distinct from each other once more, waiting.

*

On waking in the morning the first thing I do is check that the camera is still on the floor beside my bed. I pick it up, settling the heavy bag on top of the bed covers, and check the camera inside, lifting it out with great care. The tape is inside, the batteries fully charged. The camera is ready to go.

Helen is bright-eyed at the breakfast table, checking with me all the things I've already checked myself upstairs.

'You've got your camera all set up?'

'Yes, Gran.' I smile at her over a spoonful of cereal.

'The tape's all right?"

'Yes.'

'You have a full battery?'

'Yes. I can't wait Helen, I'm going as soon as I finish this.'

She gives a satisfied nod as I continue crunching my

breakfast. Bob is already out, meeting up with a few old work colleagues for a day in town. Helen tells me she's relishing the notion of having a few hours to herself.

I'm so preoccupied with making the film, thinking in circles about every detail of the day before me - the way to the woods, who I might see on the way there or the way back, what I'll film when I get there, what I'll do if there are people in the woods, and so on - that at first I don't notice the small shadows surrounding my legs as I slurp my hot chocolate.

My feet jiggle under the table and I can't rest my eyes on one thing for long. They keep darting to the back garden outside the window, then down to my food, across the table to Helen, when she always gives me a tight little smile, then back out the window at the back fence, or Bob's peas, now neatly trapped against the beanpoles in the vegetable patch.

I run back upstairs with a warm, full belly, and that is when the shadows start following, travelling with me up the stairs.

I don't see any in the rest of the house, only these ones here following my ascent to my room, and then to the bathroom, and to the bedroom again, getting ready to leave the house. Sometimes they move on ahead of me, and I take a moment to pause and note the oddness of this new development, the shadows flocking around me as I come to a halt. They've never followed me before, and they've definitely never overtaken me so that it's me following them instead. I find the spectacle entertaining and smile to myself. I'm full of smiles today.

Washed and dressed and ready to go out, I go back downstairs a few moments later to find Helen standing in the hallway, holding onto the bannister. There is a tension around her mouth and her light blue eyes that wasn't there earlier, and the tips of her hair tremble as she gives her head a tiny shake. I don't think I was supposed to see that.

'Good luck, Tom.' Her voice cracks. She gives a delicate cough and tries again, with an unconvincing smile, 'I can't wait to see what you film!' It comes out far too bright, hard against the softness in the hallway, the sun coming through the opaque glass of the fanlight.

I pretend not to notice, saying, 'Thanks Helen, bye!' and with a jingling of keys and door chains, I'm outside.

The door closes behind me and I'm alone. After the

excitement and energy of the build up to this, I feel a pressure to perform that I know is entirely in my own head. Helen is excited, but would never expect too much from me. She's simply being her usual encouraging self, but I can't stop her words becoming a booming cycle in my head and manifesting into a heaviness in my chest. My breathing gets shallower in the old familiar pattern. I should have expected this. I lean on the garden wall, steadying myself. Just calm down. It's only the Old Wood. If you don't get anything good it doesn't matter - you can go back another time and Gran won't be disappointed she wants you to have fun and CALM DOWN!

I inhale, hold the breath for a count of three, making the numbers huge in my mind to block out everything else if only for those three seconds, and blow it out, not caring if I look ridiculous. After another moment I try my own feet, and take my hand off the wall. Good, only three breaths needed this time. I walk slowly at first, concentrating hard on the pavement in front of my feet, and then pick up speed to a normal pace as I notice the shadows have followed me out of the house to surround me, walking along with me, supporting me, keeping me upright and moving in the right direction. Three or four of them are a few feet ahead, leading the way. All I have to do is follow them.

All the way to the Old Wood, across the main road and all the little side roads, around the corners and up to the gates of the wood, the shadows lead the way. I hardly think about where I'm going, instead focusing on putting one foot in front of the other, clutching my video camera bag close to my chest all the time.

The gates to the Old Wood are pretty old themselves, and ornate in a way that modern structures never are. There is a low red brick wall around this side of the wood, crumbling in places. This and the gates were a Victorian addition, now dilapidated and unloved. The centre of the gates, where they rocket up into a Gothic arch, is way above my head. They must be twice my height at their tallest, and each rail, each cross bar, is inlaid with intricate iron leaves of ivy and oak, twining around and around. Some are so worn by time and neglect they have hardly any shape left, but others have survived better, their tiny sculpted veins clear to see. At the apex of the arch, ornate lettering inlaid into the metal declares this place to be the 'Old Wood', but nobody local would need telling that.

The gates stand half open, looking like they have remained that way for decades, and I follow the shadows through. Once inside, the shadows disperse, vanishing into the wall or the trees, I can't tell, and leave me with no company but my camera.

Chapter Five

Inside the gates there are leaves scattered here and there, already fallen despite their green suppleness. The breeze is not strong enough to blow them far. They are listless and travel mere inches before resting on the soil, exhausted. All that effort of growing and greening, only to fall.

I'm more relaxed now that I'm here, though the quick departure of the shadows did unnerve me. I glance around, eyes flitting between crevices and corners in the wall, but they have definitely gone. There is no hint that they were ever here.

I can't believe I got into such a state. It's only a bunch of trees that have been here a long time. The story of the Hag is vivid in my mind from Helen's retelling of it, and I hope I can capture the same atmosphere of claustrophobia and history with my camera today.

My feet shuffle, going further into the wood. This is an old, slow place. I don't mind that the shadows are gone now that I'm getting in amongst the trees and can hear them creaking faintly in the wind. I feel safe. It was the journey here that was the problem, and I'm expecting the same sensation of being out of time, as though I don't exist, to beset me on the way home too. I mutter a brief thank you to the shadows. Regardless of what their purpose might be, they were indispensable to me on the way here, and I'm not sure I would have made it without them.

My thanks is also for the fact that I saw no-one I knew on the walk here. If anyone from school were on the path between here and my house, or on the other side of the road, my resolve would have crumbled and I would have ended up back home much earlier than expected, mumbling something to Helen about having changed my mind. They wouldn't need to speak to me or notice me. Their presence in the same pocket of air that I was moving through would have been enough; I would have been crippled with self-consciousness. That accursed freeze that is so familiar to me would have been enough to make me abandon the whole idea.

The Old Wood is on one side of the village, the houses and shops having been built on the eastern side, leaving the western side of the trees open to miles of fields and farmland that dip and rise gently to their own unique rhythm, peculiar to this part of the country.

The village is ancient, and it's thought that at one time the settlement was arranged so that it enclosed the wood, or was partly in the wood itself, with the giant beech tree as the focal point. The story of the village is hazy, and local history books are full of opinion and conjecture, but sparse with facts. All agree that it is very old, but no one knows how old, or what it was like before the brick houses were built to the east, and whatever had been to the west, if anything, had fallen away into disuse and eventually been removed altogether to make more room for growing crops and grazing sheep. The Old Wood is abandoned too, and a heavy air of neglect hangs about the branches like cobwebs waiting to be swept away.

I peer through the branches to the sky above, pale blue with sheaves of grey cloud covering the sun. I have my waterproof jacket with me, folded as small as it would go and crammed in the camera case, but I hope I won't need it.

I look around me one more time to check I'm alone before getting my camera out, leaving the bag swinging on my shoulder with only the coat in it. Once again, I check the tape and the battery, before switching the machine on and bringing it up to rest on my right shoulder. I move off, eye to the viewfinder. This part of the film is going to be my 'walking through the woods' travelogue-style introduction, before I indulge in some more artistic shots later on.

I slide each foot forward in the grass as I walk, hoping this will be enough to warn me of any big roots or fallen branches I might trip on. With my left eye shut and my right eye seeing what the camera sees, I'm relying on my feet to tell him where I'm going.

Almost straight away I stop, tutting and sighing. The camera jiggles with every step I take. I'm being careful to keep my gait even and try to glide along, but it's no good. I don't want that. I want it smooth, like a proper film. I don't want people watching to have to put up with constant bumping and sideways motions of the camera.

I lower the camera and looked around me. I'm about twenty feet from the gates, and can see the red brick wall coming away from them on either side, three feet tall, and stretching out to create a barrier between the street beyond and the wood.

Well, who's going to watch the film anyway? I'm not George Lucas. No-one knows or cares about it. From somewhere, I find a resigned smile. It's a comfort to remind myself it will most likely only ever be me, and maybe my grandparents, who see it. I raise my shoulders as high as I can get them and let them go with another sigh, a happier one this time, trying to drop all the tension stored there. 'The jiggling will be part of my film's charm,' I say out loud to myself, making myself chuckle, and raise the camera to my eye.

After a few more steps it hits me that I don't need to look through the viewfinder all the time. I can keep the camera in the same position as best I can, and look properly at where I'm going, checking through the lens occasionally to make sure I haven't veered off course, filming only blurring leaves or ground. This way it's easier to spot interesting things I can include in the film, and not get tripped up.

Perhaps I should be saying something. In travelogues the film-maker natters constantly, filling you in on history, local customs, and any native species of note. I don't want to say anything though. I want the trees to do the talking for me. They are silent, however, except for the mild swishing of their leaves. I stop, switch off the camera and turn three hundred and sixty degrees, eyes widening to take in as much as possible of my surroundings. The gate is visible behind me, but dim and distant. If I hadn't remembered which spot to look at, I could easily have missed it.

Now I'm deeper into the woods, I feel the magnitude of the trees pressing upon me, and find it impossible to resist looking up every other minute to see the sky disappearing behind the closing curtain of all those leaves. The air cools as the sun, already struggling with the clouds, has to try and get through the canopy too. I'm glad I have a long-sleeved t-shirt on.

In this wood there are ash, oak, and smaller hawthorns dotted about, growing at queer angles from the ground with spiralling trunks and thorns like sewing needles sticking out at right angles from the branches. There are beeches, limes, sycamores. I try to visualise the pages of a book on trees I got for my seventh birthday, which I devoured and memorised within weeks, but which I've forgotten almost all of now. It is in my room somewhere, but hasn't been opened for years.

I must be getting close to the centre of the wood. Ahead in the distance I can see how the trees carry on and on, with no wall to bind them on that side, and that is where the giant beech tree is, or was. They chopped it down several years ago because, and I remember the quote in the local newspaper: 'It's grown too old and big, and is a danger. The local residents' safety cannot be guaranteed while it stands. The branches are too old and delicate, it's already been struck by lightning twice, and if a branch were to get caught in a gust of wind and come down on a local child... ' The tree surgeons came and that was the end of the giant beech tree.

I wonder what the Hag thought of that. She might have made an exception in the tree surgeons' case and veered for the first time ever from her strict diet of children only, and made the wind change, freezing one of them just as he lifted his chainsaw, and dragging him, more slowly and with even greater effort than the children who were smaller and lighter, back to her bower to have the biggest feast of her life. I hope his eyeballs were extra juicy.

When I glance behind me, the gates are lost behind tree trunks and the tangles of nettles and brambles that encroach on the path and spread everywhere on the forest floor. The wood is bigger than I thought. I keep going, in a rush to get over to the other side of the wood and film back the way I've come, getting as many trees in as possible.

The trees close in and I hesitate until a gust of wind whooshes by, bending the branches above me and pushing me along. I let it move my feet and nudge me forwards. The momentum carries me for a few steps until I glance to the side, my attention caught. The wind dies down, and I see four or five shadows have joined me, a couple following in my wake and one or two, it's hard to distinguish them, moving along beside me. Maybe they were blown here. Among them, I think I can make out a fox and a cat. They must be shy. They are always hanging around at the edge of my vision, as though they don't want to be noticed.

I'm glad to see them. They've come to keep me

company, brought by the wind. Frowning, I try to focus the camera on one of them. I'm worried they might disappear after today, after I've filmed the wood, even though I am planning to come back another time to do more, and spend time here with the trees before they are destroyed. I try to film the shadows but I'm not sure what I'm capturing. They are too quick to move aside when I point the camera their way, and have that quality of fading and becoming vague when I look directly at them.

I give up and direct the camera to the trees towering over me, getting denser as I continue on. Not for the first time, I wish I had the courage to start a campaign in school, get up a petition, and rally people to the cause. That's what you do when there is something happening that you want to stop. You protest, make placards, write strongly-worded letters to people in authority, speak to people, try to win them round, try to make it stop. But not me. All that is beyond me. The thought of any kind of conversation, let alone one about a subject I have such passion for, which would thus lay me bare for yet further ridicule, is impossible to think about without wanting to run all the way home, get into bed and hide under the duvet until the thoughts stop.

Helen and Bob are concerned about it too, but are probably a bit old for protesting. It must feel to them as though a significant part of their lives is about to be decimated. They played here as children, they said, along with most of the other children in the village, despite the stories.

I try to put these thoughts to the back of my mind and focus on my goal. I need to get to the other side of the wood and find the giant beech tree stump. I glance around to check the shadows are still there.

Evidence that people do come here is more apparent the deeper into the woods I get. I flinch, a small tic that hasn't bothered me for years returning for an instant as I notice empty alcohol bottles and cans that have been thrown down wherever the imbiber happened to be when they finished. There are plastic bags in the branches, some having been there for so long there is nothing left but spectral rags flicking in the wind. There are crisp packets and chocolate wrappers. It is an endless source of puzzlement to me how people cannot bear to carry their rubbish a few yards to the nearest bin, preferring to drop it on the floor where it clearly doesn't belong. I can't imagine doing that, especially in a place like this. Too bone idle, I suppose. 'Bone idle' is a phrase Granddad often uses, and I like to use it too. It makes me think of a skeleton lounging on the sofa, ignoring all the jobs that need doing, and snoozing the day away instead. Sometimes I envy that skeleton.

Helen's face appears in my mind, worried, showing the tiny lines around her eyes. She's not as happy about me coming here as she's pretending to be, or there is something else on her mind. I've been so intent on getting here, and with the shadows distracting me, I've hardly thought about her since I last saw her standing in the hallway wringing a tissue in her hands when she thought I wasn't looking. Her brave face didn't fooled me, but I gave no response because I was being selfish, wanting to get out and get on. I resolve to ask her, and try to make sure she's okay if I can, when I get home. And to get a good film to show her.

*

It's the widest tree stump I have ever seen. Beeches can get massive, but the image in my mind as my eyes travel up and up to where those topmost branches must have been leaves me open-mouthed. It's hard to believe it was ever here, the children daring each other to climb higher and higher until one of them spied the bower the other side of the ridge, disguised among gnarly old tree roots, and in turn been espied by the Hag, whose sharp eyes missed nothing.

I look up into the hole in the air left by the branches that used to be there, delaying looking down at the stump, until I have to make myself move, willing my muscles back to life, to remove the chill that stole into them as I gazed up, up into those ghost branches. One gulp, and I return my attention to the trees that are still here, all around me.

I almost forgot about my camera, despite its weight on my shoulder. I adjust its angle and check the viewfinder. The shadows are increasing, and some go ahead of me, enticing me forward, making sure I see through the thing I came here to do. I'm only making a silly little amateur film, not delving into some ancient mystery that might be lurking under the leaves to reach out and grab me. I think again of Grandma, and how I wouldn't even be here if it were not for her encouragement and support. Her face hovers in my vision, and I'm pleased to see her, constant like that light in my room, and the shadows, making sure I'm okay.

I plod towards the stump with leaden feet, forgetting about making any attempt at gliding for the sake of the camera and concentrating on getting there. The shadows stretch out towards the stump, but I'm not sure I want to go there anymore.

I fix my eye to the viewfinder, relying on my feet to feel forwards and prevent me from tripping on any roots or bumpy bits of ground. In truth, I want to hide. Short of turning back and going home, one eye behind the viewfinder feels the safest option, and at least I can see exactly what I'm filming. The shadows are all in front of me; I take a quick glance behind to check. They pull me forwards like they did on the way here. It's as if they are cushions surrounding my every move, and if I were to stumble and fall they would lay themselves down and provide something soft for me to land on, help me back up, assure me that nobody saw, and not laugh.

The shadows are so dense around the area where the stump is that I can't distinguish one from another. Who knows how many there are. They are a blanket of darkness laid on the floor of the wood, giving the leaves and fallen branches, the moss and lost feathers, a dull, monochrome look.

I jam the viewfinder further into my eye socket. A tendril of anxiety tangles in my stomach. I feel sick. It's getting darker than I expected it would, here edging out to the other side of the wood where it sprawls away, the trees dense at first but then scattering like confetti in the wind after a wedding.

I'm eight feet from the stump when I notice something. A pinnacle of paleness appearing over the top of it. I take the camera away from my eye to look properly, but try to keep it pointed in the right direction. My eyes go big and I race around to the other side of the stump, slipping on the thick carpet of leaves. Even in this frenzy of movement, I marvel at the girth of the old beech.

There is a body. Or, at least, parts of a body. A female arm reaches up out of the leaves and rests against the tree stump. It looks frozen in the act of waving, as though no longer sure the person it was waving at is someone they recognise, after all. I edge closer, heart beating too fast. From far away thoughts come to me of breathing exercises and not getting stressed out, but they can't break through the sight of the body. I reach out, unthinking, and allow my fingertip to touch the fingertip of whoever it is who lies here. It is like stone. I recoil, my eyes roaming over the blanket of leaves, inexplicably thick. The giant beech isn't here anymore. They chopped it down four years ago. The surrounding trees at this end of the wood are not beeches, they are oaks and ashes, alders and limes. Yet they lie a foot deep, nothing but crisp orange and red beech leaves and beech nuts escaped from their spiky velvet casings, all around the stump, burying a girl.

The tip of a nose peeps out from under the leaves. It looks as frozen as the hand, but I don't touch it. There are hints of clothes; a scarf or shawl of some sort emerges and meanders away, like a brown woollen grass snake. There is the hem of a dress or a coat, it's hard to tell, grey-brown, blending in perfect camouflage with the surrounding foliage. And one boot, in a material that looks like brown suede, on its side, but with no foot in it.

Chapter Six

I hack in several ragged breaths. I should have done my breathing exercises before it got as bad at this, but I forgot about them until my chest grabbed for my attention.

I train the camera at the body and breathe in. After a few immobile seconds I breathe out again, struggling to get my pulse under control. Please let there be enough tape left. I keep recording but not moving for longer than I'm comfortable with, impatient until my breathing is less haphazard. I need evidence. No-one's going to believe me, and then the police will be called and... my mind spirals as I realise the repercussions of what I have discovered. There will be interviews and attention, cameras and questions, looks and all that unwanted scrutiny on me. I don't think I can bear it.

I film anyway, but am not so sure anymore if I am

going to show the film to anyone. Let someone else find her. Other people must come through here. The people who drop all the litter - let one of them find her and call the police and deal with all of that. Please. I film only briefly, feeling disrespectful, or as though I'm about to get caught, expecting a hand to clamp onto my shoulder at any minute.

I get shots of all the bits of her I can see coming up through the leaves, especially the hand, which I find hard to tear my attention away from. I move around her with nimble steps, crouching to get as close as I dare, wading through the leaves to film the few millimetres of nose cresting, the shawl breaking, and back up to get all of her into frame. My eyes return again and again to the hand. It must have only stopped waving a second before I saw the tip of the forefinger from the other side of the stump. Following the natural line of the direction her hand is facing, I look over my shoulder, already knowing what I'll see; the ridge towards the edge of the wood, beyond which the stories say the bower lurks. I film the hand some more, but feel queasy again, and have to remind myself that this is not some fascinating artefact in a museum, but a real human being, dead at my feet.

The straps and zips fight with my fumbling fingers as I shove the camera back in its bag, eyes flitting back to her hand. I have to keep checking it's still there, I'm not imagining it.

Two splats of rain hit my arm, as though a child high up in the ghost branches is spitting on me.

Clutching the camera bag to my chest, fingers digging into the green canvas, I run. I turn away from the body and the vast empty space high up, once occupied by majestic arching beech branches, and do not look back once. I can't bear it a second longer. The sudden, sharp rainstorm jolts me, and it's all too real.

This is not some daydream. I'm getting soaked, the heaving raindrops going straight through the thin t-shirt I was so glad of before. I run, following the path I took here, my breathing shallow and noisy. I pull the camera back further into my chest to try and ease the discomfort inside, and think about getting my anorak out, but it's too late for that: I'm already drenched, and the camera landed on top of it when I shoved it into the bag. The anorak appears in my mind's eye, crumpled and squashed, forgotten about and neglected, and I feel a hollow ache in my throat, close to tears.

The rain splashing the leaves sends up a green scent that fills my nostrils. The humidity closes in, making running harder, like I have to cut through the air to get out. Getting back to the gates takes longer than all the time I've been in the woods, I'm sure. They are so far away, but I won't stop until I get there, even if my chest protests with every step, and the heady pungency of the greenery makes my head throb.

It's not a physical breathing condition I have: it's panic attacks. If I don't control them quickly enough with the breathing exercises Helen - motherly, kind Helen, alone in the house - taught me I can be laid up for the rest of the day, exhausted by the turning in my mind, endless thoughts repeating, and the physiological responses they wring from my body.

I stumble past the trees, weaving around the trunks, avoiding the worst of the brambles and nettles instinctively, but not caring if they catch me. What is, after all these years, an automatic response kicks in, making me try to slow my breathing, but it is impossible while I'm belting through the woods, my only intent to get to the gates as fast as I can. The trees lean in, bending lower over me. Their leaves close in on my hair. The gates, which I can finally see, recede from me instead of growing closer, and the trees observe me in their slow, passive way, making note not to let me in next time, passing messages with the blackbirds and tits that thread them together. Stop, stop, stop, stop, stop, and run.

 I reach the gate and cling to a slick railing, like a boy out at sea in choppy water, hanging on so he doesn't drown. I hold on tight. One of the little iron leaves digs its sharp edges into my fingers, making me wince and draw in a sharp breath. The branches spin above me, the ground moves like quicksand. Never letting go, I reach for the next upright railing in the gate with my other hand, juggling the camera bag which, rather than my beloved machine, has become a cumbersome weight, pulling me forwards and getting in the way. Five times I pass the bag from one arm to the other, never daring to put it down, forgetting all about the strap I could so easily utilise, and grip the next railing with my free hand, moving around the unyielding ironwork until I'm on the other side, my feet half on the grass of the woods, and half on the pavement, and I can stop.

I turn away from the gates and the wood, and that's when I remember the shadows. They disappeared when I got to the stump, vanishing the second I saw that pale finger, beckoning.

I move a little way along the pavement, and sit on the wall, camera bag still clutched at my chest, but loosening my grip. Breathe in. I look around as I count, one... two... three, trying to appear nonchalant in case there is anyone about. Glancing up and down the street, I blow the air out until it's all gone. Again, keep going.

A man comes out of a house across the road and runs to his car, an old Ford Capri like I'm going to have when I'm old enough, gets in and drives past. He gives no sign that he saw me. A family are crossing the road, bundled in raincoats and trying to keep umbrellas up, too preoccupied to bother about a boy sitting on a wall, apparently doing nothing.

The rain has almost stopped, nothing left of it but regular slow dollops on the road. A faint tinkling sound tells me the door of the corner shop has been opened, and out come a couple of people I recognise from school. I hold my breath, but they turn in the opposite direction, walking away from me. I will not move until they are round the corner and out of sight. Breathe out.

After a further moment or two spent trying to be invisible and getting my breathing back to normal, trying to think of nothing but that, I rise, jeans more soggy that ever from the wall. I'm conscious they are sticking to my bum and legs as I walk along. The rain stops completely, leaving only fat drips to come down from the eaves of buildings and leaves of trees. My shirt sticks to my back.

I concentrate on getting home, not getting run over, and trying to keep my breathing normal and my shoulders as relaxed as I can. There are no shadows to help me on my journey this time.

*

I'm not sure of my angles. I was shaky and shocked when I was trying to film. I can't guess from which edge of the screen that waving arm will emerge.

I watch, the tape whirring in the machine, the images crisp and rendered in a rainbow of greys. The camera bumps around but I do my best not to get irritated by it. At times I forgot to point it at anything in particular, and all that's on the screen is blurring leaves, scraps of litter, or the sky. At other times I managed to frame the trees quite well. It's not a complete disaster. I'm occupying my mind until the tape gets to the part I need to see, close to the end. I watch, trying to take in every inch of the screen at the same time, not daring to blink.

Five minutes later I shut my eyes tight, taking in long noisy breaths. When I open them I rewind the film and watch it again, all the way through. And then one more time.

There's nothing there.

I watch the tape seven times in total, after rushing past Helen, who is hovering in the hallway as if she's been there all day, full of questions about how did it go, did I have fun, and what do I want for tea? I grab the camera out of its bag as soon as the door to my bedroom shuts behind me, trying to be careful but in too much of a rush. I remove the tape and put it into the video player before I've even switched the machine on, or indeed plugged it in at the wall.

It's all so laborious, all I want to do is see what's on the tape, and I have to faff about with leads and cables, plug the TV and the video in, switch them on and wait for them to warm up. I glare as the screen bobbles with snow and cssshhhhhhhhes at me. I'm fond of the white noise usually, but today it's in the way and taking too long. It's the sound of nothing and everything all at once, and beautiful for that, but not what I want to hear in this moment.

I tap my fingers on the floor where I'm crouched on my haunches, ready for action. There isn't a stand or a table for my TV, it simply sits on the floor of my room, and I sit on the floor opposite it, or lay on the bed if I'm not too bothered about seeing the screen properly, when I'm watching. The video player sits next to it. They take up too much space, but I treasure them so much the idea of keeping them in the spare room, as Helen suggested when I first got them, is unthinkable.

The screen flickers and I press rewind on the video player. The tape spools, getting higher and higher pitched until it screeches to a stop. Hesitant after all my impatience, I press play. I want to take it all in, absorb every pixel, miss nothing. I play the tape over and over, searching more intently every time, looking with all my might. After the seventh time, I leave the tape in the machine, not bothering to rewind it, and retreat to my bed, where I sit on my pillows looking out of the window to the street below, a quiet cul-de-sac lined with lime trees that litter the pavement with their bitty seeds every autumn and mess up the roofs of the cars.

My heart thumps as if I'm running through the forest again, and I go through the motions of my breathing exercises automatically to calm myself. The fallen leaves caught in a vortex and swirling around our tiny front garden transfix me.

Nothing there. A few ash and oak leaves, fallen early after a dry summer, twigs, a couple of fallen branches, and that is all. No beech leaves, no beech nuts, and no arm, hand, nose, scarf, clothing or boots. None of it is there. Not on the tape, anyway.

I spring from the bed and take two large strides across the room to catch up my camera from where I left it on the floor, and sit back on the bed, facing in towards the room, back against the wall beside the window. I need to be holding it. I glower at the television screen, which glowers blackly back, and cradle the camera in my lap.

I try to formulate what I'll say to Helen and Bob. My mind is foggy. It's obvious I can't tell them what I saw, especially since the evidence of the video tape contradicts it so completely. There is no evidence.

I also know with equal certainty that I will have to go back for another look. If the body is there, or if it is not, will decide what I do after that. I string together a story about how I was really getting into my filming but it started to rain, so I packed my camera away and ran home. Feasible, and very close to the truth. I'll just be sure to sound happy about it, as though nothing odd or unusual happened, and I'll make sure I don't mention the shadows again. They are already giving me concerned glances when they think I can't see, since I was foolish enough to ask about those.

Downstairs, the story comes easily and they don't ask any awkward questions. Something about Helen's expression while I'm talking worries me. She had the same look when I blurted out that silly question about the shadows last week. She says all the correct, reassuring things, but there is a subtle change in her expression, the tiny lines around her mouth become more defined, her eyebrows set where they are, not mobile like normal.

All evening, the more I try to keep the conversation light and natural, the more laboured and unnatural it feels. The Generation Game finishes and I turn to Gran the same way I did when I asked her to tell me the story of the Hag in the Woods. She is caught off guard, absorbed in her own thoughts, and flinches but composes herself immediately.

'Gran,' I start, trying to sound gentle and relaxed, unsuccessfully. 'I think,' I chew my bottom lip. 'I think... something about the wood.' I look up at those clear pale guileless eyes, which I've inherited through my mother's line. 'There's something you're not telling me.' I clamp my mouth shut and look away from her. I'm not sure I want to hear whatever she might say. After the events of the day, it might be too much, but this tension between us is unbearable and I'll get no sleep if I don't at least ask. Maybe I've ensured no sleep tonight, now that I have asked.

Helen looks down at her hands. She's spinning her engagement ring round and round on her finger, a nervous gesture I recognise from other times she's been uncomfortable. She doesn't speak for a long time, while I watch from under my lashes for any sign of what she might be thinking. I've never seen her this guarded, and the expression on her face makes me regret asking. She's almost squirming. Eventually, having apparently reached a decision, she looks up. Her face is still tense but I can see she's making efforts to relax it and to appear her usual calm, capable self.

'It's nothing Tom, I think I'm just upset about the developers coming to the wood, that's all. Sorry if I've alarmed you.' She looks down, as though it's her turn to be afraid of my reaction. I know in my gut that what my trustworthy, earnest, dependable grandma just said is not the truth, or not the full truth, but it is clear this is not a matter she will be pushed on.

'Okay,' I say, relieved the conversation, if you could call it that, is over even if I didn't learn anything. I summon a small smile to show I'm not upset. I'm hesitant to say anything else in case my tongue runs away with me, which it does sometimes, and I blurt out everything that happened in the woods today. I chew at my lip until I realise what I'm doing, and catch Gran looking at me, curiosity in her eyes.

'Well, I think I'll go up to bed now.' It sounds too formal, like I'm a guest in her house.

She looks like she might say more so I wait, but she remains silent. I'm desperate to ask but I don't. The conversation is so strained and stretched it will surely snap if either of us press further.

I go upstairs, taking them one at a time for once instead of bounding up taking two at once. I cannot shake the atmosphere of there being something bad the adults all know about and are trying to protect me from. I remember the feeling well from when my parents died. All the grown ups were so at pains to not further upset me, they ended up doing exactly that with their reticence to talk about it. It follows me up the stairs, the fuzzy creep of that withheld knowledge, and I feel at once patronised and protected.

I'm across the room and sitting on the edge of my bed before I remember the tape is still in the machine. Maybe I was mistaken. Maybe I somehow filmed the wrong side of the stump, and not the side the woman was on. Maybe, as I got flustered and my breathing started doing that annoying thing it does, I got totally confused and didn't actually point the camera at the body at all.

The video player sits innocently on the floor. My unfocused eyes roam over its silver surface as though looking for clues. That girl, woman, whatever she was, might still be there, the tip of her nose and her waving hand getting covered with dew now that the sun has gone down, like the grass and moss all around her.

I have to watch the tape again, but glean no further information from it. All there is each time are the things I grow tired of seeing, because they are not what I'm looking for. A huge tree stump with deep craggy rivulets running up and down the bark, roots laid on the ground, six or eight feet long, before vanishing into the earth like the tentacles of a great Kraken in the ocean. Two fallen branches drifted across from other trees. A few tufts of grass, scattered leaves from other trees, and not much else. No thick velvet carpet of beech nut cases, no mass of orange beech leaves forming drifts against the stump. And no sign of any body; human, animal or otherwise. Even if I was in a complete muddle, which I know I wasn't, and filmed the wrong side of the stump, the leaves would still be there. The tip of that cold, white finger beckoning me is nowhere to be seen. She is simply not there.

I get into bed. The light from the street light outside stretches across the ceiling, constant and reliable. The camera is once again tucked down by the side of the bed like a beloved pet.

Drifting off to sleep, my blinks become longer and my breathing slower, and I have the idea that I should rewind the tape and tape over it next time. That would be the practical thing to do. There is nothing of any use on it, nothing with any artistic or practical merit. But, in the part of me that I also use for making decisions - the part that gives me hunches and tells me when Grandma is keeping something from me - I am sure that would be the wrong thing to do. That dread sensation, when my whole six year old world was flipped upside down like the old Allegro my parents perished in - the way my heart seemed to stop for a long time, until it hurt in my chest and I was aware of it beating again - returns for a moment, and I sink lower into the mattress, shying away from it.

I look at the light from the street lamp. It encompasses my own ceiling light in the room, laying its luminescence across the thick wire it dangles from and the dark striped lampshade, as though trying to switch it on. You have no light? Here, have some of mine.

It was years until I started to properly grieve for my parents. As young as I was, I felt it was my job to be strong for all the other people who were affected by it. It didn't occur to me for a long time that it was me who needed the support, and the patience, and it took even longer for me to see that I had been receiving it all along. A sort of mythology grew up around Mum and Dad, the version of events that the grown-ups deemed suitable for a six year old to stomach almost blotting out the reality. That's how it happens, I suppose. That is how ordinary or extraordinary events become myth and folklore. People tell the stories.

The film I took in the woods, as deceitful as it was, I took at the time that I saw the body, and I worry that erasing the tape might also erase my true memory of the day and what I saw. As grim as it is, I want it to be real, because if it's not that means I'm seeing things, or there are ghosts, or some other phenomenon I can't explain.

My eyes close for thirty seconds, but snap open again, going straight to the light on the ceiling out of habit, as another thought pulls at me. Maybe the shadows did something! They were keen for me to go there, helping me all the way. If it were not for them I probably would have chickened out and not even got as far as the gate of the Old Wood in the first place. I have not seen one since the wood. They have a gift for forming shapes, and morphing, changing. Maybe they somehow conjured the body. Maybe they are still out there in the Old Wood, pretending to be a dead girl's body and lots of beech leaves. No, I'm going crazy. My eyes close.

In my dream, the girl waves to me like a friend. She smiles, pleased to see me, her long auburn hair falling in a wave over her shoulders. She has creamy white skin with pinkish blotches on her cheeks from the cold. Crystal blue eyes, too clear. Her clothes are old-fashioned. She doesn't have much money, I can tell, and probably makes most of her clothes herself, or likely has them made for her by somebody who loves her. They are of hard wearing brownish grey fabric and look warm. There is a wide scarf around her shoulders of rough wool in a dark red, almost brown. Her boots keep the damp earth from her feet, protecting with a layer of what looks like suede.

We have arranged to meet. She has something to tell me that I want to hear. There are no shadows here, but I saw them before, pressed up against the outside of the perimeter wall. They look like they are eavesdropping, or hiding, or both. They fear to come in while the girl is alive, shrinking instead against the red bricks and quivering like branches reflected in a rushing river. Her smile broadens as I approach. Her age is hard to determine, she could be in her teens, could be older, could be a bit younger. She is taller than me and gazes down at me as a beneficent goddess might, or a kindly mother.

She enfolds me in her arms as soon as I'm close enough to reach. Her body chills me, she is like ice. Her voice comes from far away, but I can hear her perfectly. It is low, intimate, inside my head, and all around in the trees at the same time. I know no-one else can hear it. All she says is, 'Beware of the shadows,' before smiling a smile that this time fades around the edges so that it is sad and brave, with no cheer left in it, and then becomes flat like the line on an echo cardiogram when a person's heart stops beating. She retreats, the warmth returning to my limbs as she removes her frozen touch and turns, disappearing too fast, not walking but gliding over the ridge beyond which the Hag's bower rests. She's gone.

Chapter Seven

Next morning I'm eager to be out and back in the wood. If there is a body out there, I need to do something about that, so I have to go and check. Also, I want to find out what's happened to the shadows, disappearing so fast like that after delivering me to the stump. I have a strong hunch that now I have seen what they wanted me to see, their purpose is done and they have gone back to wherever they came from. That's what shadows should do, I suppose. They're not supposed to hang around all the time shape-shifting through day and night. They are meant to be transient things, coming and going according to what light source there is, and growing and shrinking according to how far away that source is, and at what angle. I chuckle to myself at the idea of telling the shadows off for getting it wrong. But the laughter can't quite release the tension that's been with me since yesterday morning, and I grow serious again. I get out of bed, running a hand over the top of my head to dislodge my hair where it feels stuck in an unnatural style. It makes no difference to what it looks like, the brown waves will still stick up in all directions until I can get a bit of water and a comb to it, but it makes me feel less stale.

I won't be getting any help on the way to the Old Wood today: the shadows are gone for good. I don't understand why I'm so bereft at the thought, except that they were almost like friends for a while. My instincts tell me I have seen the last of them. I do feel braver than yesterday, simply because I made the same journey the day before. It is all mapped out in my mind; which streets to take, where to turn, the exact position of the gates to the wood. I know to avoid going past the corner shop in case those boys are there and see me this time. And I know to expect to see a body resting beyond the giant beech stump. It will not be a horrific surprise this time. I'm not looking forward to it, going more out of a sense of duty than anything else, but feel better prepared than I was yesterday.

I eject the tape from the video player where it has

slept all night, fighting the urge to watch it one more time. The girl is not going to have materialised on the tape overnight. In fact, I don't want to see the tape again as it only confounds what I saw, and that annoys me. There's still plenty of space on the tape, I only used about half yesterday, so I put it back into the camera, planning to start today's filming where yesterday's finished. Rummaging in a drawer, I find another blank tape to squeeze into the camera bag too, in case this one runs out.

I stop in the middle of the room in my pyjamas, looking at the camera. Then in a rush of impatience I lift it, remove yesterday's tape and throw it onto the duvet where it irritates me by refusing to sink down through the eiderdown into oblivion, instead floating on the top, insolent. I ignore it, turning away to put the fresh tape into the camera. Today is a new day, a fresh start. After checking the battery has plenty of life, and tinkering with one or two of the buttons, I lay the camera down on the bed while I go downstairs for breakfast.

*

I pause at the gates to the Old Wood, looking up and

down the street, in the direction I've come in, and through the gates. No shadows. I haven't seen one since I was at the beech stump yesterday. They have abandoned me. Fortunately, today I'm stronger and braver than yesterday and did not need their assistance to get me here. Maybe that's why they've gone; they sense that I no longer need them. Or, as I was thinking last night, maybe they have finished with me in a rather more sinister way. It is funny sometimes, how something can be both helpful to you and detrimental at the same time. The shadows felt like that, especially after the dead girl's warning in my dream last night. 'Beware of the shadows.' Well, the shadows are gone, but I'm staying alert and wary in case they should reappear, although I'm not sure what I'm supposed to do about it if they do. They are shadows. I can't grab them or run away from them. They would chase me, overtake me, lead me to some other place and show me some other thing I don't want to see.

Satisfied that there are no shadows around, except for the naturally occurring one springing from my feet to lay across the pavement, as the sun is out this morning, I go through the gates. There is no hesitating this time - I make straight for the other side of the wood, where the stump is.

The air is lighter in the woods today. The cloying atmosphere from yesterday has gone, and the sun sends spokes of light through the branches overhead to warm the air and make it less gloomy. With effort I ignore the rubbish and debris scattered along the narrow track that the few people who visit here have made through the grass. But I do glance up at the plastic bags hanging like shrouds from some of the branches overhead, forlorn even as they are lit up from behind by the sun. They almost look like Chinese lanterns today, if I squint a bit.

I fix my eyes on where I'm going and stride through the ferns, stepping over large exposed roots and the occasional fallen branch. I cling to my camera, holding it to my chest as before, as if it might save me if anything untoward happens. My feet scuff the ground far more roughly than they did yesterday. I've forgotten any sensibilities I might have had about not causing even the smallest injury to this place. It still has a sacred and portentous air, but I'm in too much of a rush to get to the stump to worry about that. I'm scared I will lose my bottle if I don't get it over with quickly, or that the shadows might realise they have forgotten something and be back.

I could swear it's a much shorter distance to the stump than yesterday; I'm there already. I come to an abrupt halt and wobble on my feet. Here we are. I take long steady strides all around the stump, my eyes never leaving it and the spread of ground at its base. I study it as I studied the tape last night in my room, but it's only a stump. A massive stump, yes, it must have taken some chopping down, that giant of a beech, but just a stump nonetheless.

I pull out my camera and switch it on, thinking that what I record might once more be the opposite of what I actually see. The body, so blatantly absent from the scene before me, might appear on the tape when I watch it later, with its scarf and boot and tip of nose poking through the leaves. I film all around, from every angle I can think of, far calmer than yesterday, and making sure I capture the stump from every side, from ground level, and from eye level. I film every crevice in the bark and stand on tiptoes to film the circles visible on its top where it was hacked down. Countless circles repeating all the way to the edge in thin wavering lines, some dark, some lighter.

I creep round and round the stump, and once I think I've caught all I can of that, I turn my attention to the roots, which I couldn't see much of yesterday due to the multitude of beech leaves covering them. I follow them, tracing their journeys as they meander for yards away from the stump, tapering until they dip under the ground, gone to earth like frightened rabbits. After this I get some footage of the rest of the wood, looking out from the stump back the way I came to where the gate is, forever half open, with its red brick arms stretched out to encircle the trees.

Lowering the viewfinder from my eye, I let the camera hang upside down in my hand, and look around. The sun lightens the leaves of the canopy from behind, making them glow. A squirrel scampers away up a nearby trunk and vanishes into the branches. It reappears, high up on the end of a branch, and leaps across to the neighbouring tree, bushy tail straight out behind it as it flies, and curling on landing. Two crows are having a conversation above my head: one on the top branch of a sycamore beside me, the other somewhere over the other side of the wood where I can't see it.

'Hello,' I say. I always say hello to crows.

There is one thing left to do before I can go. I had planned to do this yesterday, but events got out of my control before I had a chance. I balance on one of the thick roots of the stump, teetering on the roundness of it, and walk up it tightrope-style. I clamber up, one knee first, and then a few hops on the other foot as my innards curdle at the thought that maybe I'm too weak, too ill-practised at climbing trees, or climbing anything, to be able to get my sweaty fourteen year old body onto the top. But then the other knee is up, and I grit my teeth, shuffling on my knees to get nearer the centre of the stump, and stand up.

I turn and look back towards where the gate is. The extra height that short climb has given me makes all the difference to the view. The trees fan out before me, and I'm delighted to see that from this angle, somehow all signs of man ever having been here are invisible. The perimeter wall is too far away to see anyway, but the crisp packets, carrier bags, and the rest of the things that people couldn't be bothered to find a bin for are all hidden on the other side of the ferns and the undergrowth, or the thick branches, or in shadow created by the thin points of light coming from the sun.

I am triumphant standing here, like a Lord surveying my kingdom. I raise the camera to my eye and try for what I had planned all along when I first wanted to come here. A wide sweeping pan across the woods, left to right, keeping the camera level, parallel with the ground, and then right to left with the camera looking up, up to capture those long arching branches, the sunlight behind the leaves, maybe one of those crows, before finally coming down to the centre, looking directly back towards the gate to show the arrangement of the trees. Satisfied and smiling to myself, I begin my descent down the stump, every bit as awkward and clumsy as the ascent was. Feet back on the ground, I put the camera into its bag, and without so much as a glance around, stride back towards the gates.

*

Back home, I'm elated to have something to show Helen and Bob. I put the tape into the main video player in the living room, at their request, and it is unremarkable, if pleasant. From their response, it is exactly as they expected. I didn't check it before showing it to them. That idea I had in the woods that the body would somehow appear on the tape when it had not been there in real life this time was ridiculous. I'm so relieved I didn't see the body this time, I find I don't care so much if there is something odd about the tape. If there is, we can deal with it all together, as a family. But it is all there exactly as I recorded it, with nothing out of place or unusual.

That evening is unusual, however, in that I enjoy it. Sunday nights are normally full of dread for me. The threat of school the next day fills my mind as I stay in my room watching TV, or forcing myself to get my homework finished. But this Sunday evening I stay in the living room with my grandparents after dinner, watching a hospital drama set in the fifties that I confuse myself by not hating. I might watch it every week.

'Did you like my tape, Gran?' I ask after the show has finished.

'I did, Tom, I think you did a nice job of capturing the woods, especially that panning shot at the end.' She sweeps her arms from one side of the room to the other, in case I might not get what she means. 'That was super. I haven't been in the wood for years, but you've made me want to pay a visit now.' She smiles warmly at me, but I feel my own smile fade from my lips. I hadn't considered the possibility that Helen or Bob would want to go to the woods themselves. I don't want to risk them seeing the body or the shadows. I can't tell her what to do, but I don't want her going there without me. Aside from anything else, it's my place, and if anything did happen, I couldn't forgive myself for letting her go on her own, or with Bob. I have to be there if they are going.

'You must take me with you!' I give a little laugh at the end, in case it came out sounding too abrupt.

'You really like it there, don't you? It's such a pity about these developers. I don't like to think of all those lovely old trees you filmed there coming down within the year.'

'Within the year?'

'That's what it said on the news earlier. The contracts have been finalised and work will begin within the year. So, we haven't got long to go and see those old trees if we want to. I know they said within the year, but I don't see they've got any reason to hang about. There's a lot more money in houses than in trees and they'll want to get cracking sooner rather than later, I should think, before the bad weather.'

'We should all go next weekend.' I try to sound encouraging.

Bob, who until now has given every impression of not listening, looks up.

'Next week? I have golf next week, you know.'

'Only on the Sunday. We could go on the Saturday,' Gran says.

Bob purses his lips, looking back at the television. He is not all that interested in the Old Wood, although if pushed he will admit that he far prefers the trees to these horrible new-build houses they keep putting up everywhere. Tacky little boxes, he calls them.

'Well, we'll see.' He shuffles down in his chair, arms folded, indicating that this is his last word on the subject.

Helen and I exchange a glance. We are used to Bob's more boring nature meaning we usually end up doing things together, without him. Helen gives me that small warm smile again, reassuring me that at least she will go with me if Bob doesn't want to.

By mid-week, I know I don't want to take Helen to the woods with me. Most of all, I'm worried about the shadows coming back. I don't want to see them ever again, and my concern is that they might be disturbed from wherever they are currently slumbering by any fresh interest in the wood.

*

I'm in the library at lunch time, one of my haunts around the school where I can be sure I will be left alone, talking to myself. I do this a lot. I don't mean to, it just happens. I think everyone does it, anyway. It helps me to think and formulate things in my mind. Sometimes, I'm walking down the street and don't realise I'm doing it until someone else comes into view, looking at me in that curious way, and I clamp my mouth shut, gazing off to the side. What? No, you didn't hear any voices. There's only me here, see. It doesn't matter if I'm in my room - I can natter to myself all the time, coming up with plans for writing and films I'll make. The quiet of the library closes in on me, making me realise I'm doing it again: repeating conversations with other pupils that morning; what they said, my response, trying out different inflections, how I would say it differently next time. Except I don't, of course. I'm the same as always, and do this analysis afterwards, alone, in a never-ending spiral. I will my mouth to stay shut.

After lurking at my favourite corner table for a few minutes, pretending to be busy making notes in a tatty exercise book, I seize my moment to be brave and speak to the librarian for the first time. She is in her fifties or early sixties - I'm rubbish at guessing ages - and permanently clothed in a dark-coloured long pleated skirt and a white blouse. Her hair is loose and curled like mine, but longer and blonder. She always wears the same pink cameo brooch over the top button of her blouse, under her chin. When not reading, her face appears distracted, as though not sure what to do with itself if not concentrating on a book.

In a rush of over confidence, I slide the exercise book into my bag and stride across the library to stand in front of her desk. She doesn't look up straight away. She never does, I've noticed. If anyone wants her to listen to them they have to wait until she has finished the sentence she is reading. I wait, watching her eyes move left and right. I know the 'I'm ignoring you' determination in her face; it's an expression that must often show on mine, too. It's a long sentence. I shift my weight from one foot to the other, confidence fading, thinking about leaving without asking, when she looks up with an over-bright smile, not saying anything. Okay, she's noticed me. No escaping now.

'Ahem,' I croak, trying to clear my throat and smile back at her. 'Hello. I was wondering if you might have any books about The Hag in the Woods?' Good grief, so formal. The heat creeps up from under my collar, stealing its way up my neck. Great, blushing too. I can't stand the inquisitive look she's giving me any longer and glance away towards the door, thinking if I run for it, leg it out of the library, she'll think I'm an odd child, definitely, but it would prevent any further embarrassment.

'The Hag in the Woods?' she says. Oh god, she doesn't know what it is. I'm going to have to explain the whole thing. I look down at her desk, smoother and darker than the others in the room, not having been attacked by quite so many pens and compasses over the years.

'Er, yes. The local story about The Hag in the Woods,' I mumble. This is excruciating. I dare myself to look at her face, and am amazed to find her smiling, looking interested. Encouraged, I go on. 'Er, I wondered if there might be anything about the story, or... anything. Um, studies, or theories, or, erm, the story itself?' My hands are waving about listlessly as I speak, and with great effort I make them stop and float down to my sides. Keep still.

'Well, yes, I should have something, surely!' Her voice is much more lively and warm than I expected. I've seldom heard her speak before, and then only at a great distance. I never listen properly anyway when she's talking to someone else, being too absorbed in whatever I'm studying.

She rises, the movement giving me a jolt. I had a notion that she might not be a real person after all, which would have saved my embarrassment, but this getting up and walking about confounds that idea. She leads me to the far wall of the library, the Local Studies section, and walks her fingers sideways along the spines of the books, humming to herself. At length her fingers stop on a slim volume, pulling it out from between a book about local geography and another one called, 'All the way to Annisthorpe'.

'Here!' She holds it up. It's one of the thinnest books I've ever seen. In fact, it's a pamphlet. She hands it to me. 'I don't think there are any more I'm afraid. Just let me...' her fingers trip along, tapping each spine, ticking them off as relevant or not. I look at the book. The cover proclaims it to be 'The Annisthorpe Log Book.' Weird title, as if Annisthorpe is a ship.

'Ah, no, nothing else at the moment, I'm afraid. If you have a chance you should try the local library too. They would be more likely to have something.' She turns to me, a look of disappointment on her face. 'I thought we had more than that.' She gestures to the book I'm holding, as though apologising for it.

'It's okay, thank you.' I'm so relieved the conversation is over that I don't care how few books the library has on the subject. I imagine going to the local library and having a similar conversation with the librarian there, and shudder inwardly. I carry the book over to my original spot, feeling ludicrous for not sitting at the table closest to where she found it. No, it has to be this one in the corner, sorry. The librarian glides back to her position too, receding once more into the background of the day, her usual habitat, and silence falls once more.

The book consists of A4 sheets folded and stapled together. They have been meticulously typed, but remind me more of a school magazine produced by pupils than a proper book. I get comfortable, taking out my exercise book and pen, and flick through The Annisthorpe Log Book. I'm grateful there is an index - it's the first thing I find, flicking from back to front (I have a pet hate for non-fiction books that don't have an index), although it's hard to imagine it being necessary for such a small book, and indeed it only has half a page of entries. I then start from the beginning and study the contents page, which I am also pleased to see.

I run my forefinger down the list of contents, stopping as soon as I see the word 'Hag'. There it is. Turning to page 17, as indicated, I begin to read. The book is written in the sort of extravagant language that I would get marked down for in English class, by someone who appeared to be enjoying themselves far too much. It's the sort of book I might write if I ever felt the inclination, although I hope I would do a better job with the presentation and find more to fill its pages. The language and exuberance of the author make me imagine that Helen might have written it, and I can't resist checking the front cover to see if her name is there. I smile to myself at the thought, but no, it's not by my grandma, but by someone called E. Eddison. I read.

'The people of Annisthorpe tell of a terrible old Hag who lives in the woods adjacent to the village. She is said to be a normal sized old woman, until angered when she inexplicably grows to three times her previous height and devours all who lie in her path.' This is surpassing even Helen's version. 'She is pure black in colour and shines with an inner demonic light said to come straight from the core of the earth itself.' I chuckle at the description. 'She drips an acrid tar-like substance from every extremity and when she moves her head, it flies out in all directions from her hideous hair, instantly killing anyone it touches.' Oh dear. I'm tempted to shut the book. This Eddison person is getting a bit carried away, using the local legend as a spring board for his own bizarre imaginings. I give him one more chance. 'Wherever she treads, the grounds recoils and nothing grows there forever more.'

Well, this is fun, but not telling me much, except that E. Eddison has an over-active imagination. I close the book and take it back to where it came from, squeezing it in between the same two books. Going back to my corner, where I left my bag and book, I ponder a different approach. When I get back to the desk my bottom rests on the chair for only a second before I'm up again, in another incautious rush of confidence, and striding across to where the librarian sits, reading. I hesitate for a long moment, standing in front of her desk as she once more emerges before me as a real person I'm going to have to speak to, instead of the anonymous librarian on the other side of the room.

'Do you have anything about shadows?' I could have put that better, but it's out now. I squirm at the librarian, who repeats, 'Shadows?' with a quizzical expression.

I try to sound sure of what I'm talking about, 'Yes. Er, shadows and how they work. Physics, I suppose. But how it can go wrong sometimes.' Oh dear. I shift my gaze sideways, thinking once more about escaping. There is no way to frame it to make it sound like a normal question.

'Physics!' She sounds relieved to have something

more familiar to grasp onto, and smiles again, showing her wonky teeth. Her voice lights up the part of the library we're in like a desk lamp. 'Well the physics books are over here.' She walks deeper into the room, in a different direction from before. 'Let's have a look!' she calls over her shoulder, as I realise I'm still standing in front of her desk, and rush to catch up despite every instinct telling me to run from the room.

I try to make myself smaller as I walk, hunching my shoulders, looking down, pretending nonchalance, so as not to draw further attention to myself. I would be ecstatic if the librarian turned around to find no-one there, so I could make my escape in sudden invisibility and never darken her door again. As it is I will have to go through all the motions of pretending that yes, indeed, I am looking for a physics book when that's not what I want in the slightest. It's not possible to explain to her what I actually want to look up without telling her about the shadows. It's better to leave it. They are probably gone for good. I should forget about them instead of brooding. Thinking too much, that's my trouble. I stand beside her, not really listening as she runs through the library's scant physics books looking for something about shadows. Mercifully, as she is pulling a book out for me, the bell goes for the end of lunch break, and I make my excuses and leave.

I try my best to forget about the shadows, but find the act of trying to forget about them only makes me think about them more. I'm fixating on the warning about them from the woman in my dream. Sitting in maths class, I shake my head. It's a tiny action from side to side. I'm trying to get rid of the thoughts, to get some respite, but this is enough to instigate much giggling among the other pupils. They never need much encouragement to see me as the class loon, and soon have to be hushed by the teacher. I try not to care.

Their laughter has the effect of bringing me back fully to the room, which is a good thing. The teacher might ask me a question at any time - they can't resist trying to catch children out who look like they might be daydreaming. The urge to get out into the fresh air and draw in long breaths of it is immense, but I don't do that. Bursting out of the classroom to heave in great breaths of air would only increase the other pupils' mirth and probably get me a detention as well. Instead, I do what I always do; sit in silence with my head down, trying to get my brain to work out the maths problem in front of me and not everything else that's going round and round in my stupid head.

This maths lesson - double maths on a Wednesday afternoon, the No Man's Land of the week - feels like it will never end. It's too warm. The year is turning into autumn, but everyone's wearing short sleeves and distracted expressions. The low afternoon sun comes straight in at us through the windows. Some children have to shield their eyes in order to see the paper in front of them. One boy raises his hand to ask the teacher if he can close the blind, but all he gets is a withering look and a threat of detention if he speaks again. The sun will help us focus on our work, the teachers says. Maybe he's so dazzled by it that he can't see us, shifting in our chairs, fanning ourselves, grabbing the fronts of our shirts at the neck and flapping them in and out to try and cool down. Teachers can be very stupid sometimes.

The heat prickles on my chest and back, tiny spikes of fire in my armpits making the sweat run down my sides. I hope my deodorant holds out, dreading the creation of yet another thing for the others to tease me about. I subtly moved my head to the side and inhale. It seems to be doing okay, thank goodness.

That sun never lets up. I move to scratch at my head, fingers fumbling through thick curly hair to find my scalp. My arm is like a robot's, such is my self-consciousness, always tensed ready for the next jibe, the next laugh at whatever innocent movement or expression I perform. I'm amazed how other children can find things I'm not even aware of doing such a rich source of amusement. Now the simple act of scratching my head becomes something to agonise over for minutes before I dare move, and worry and niggle about after the deed is done, and try to do without moving at all if possible to avoid drawing any attention to myself.

All afternoon the sun remains, lowering but never finding a cloud to hide behind to provide a tiny bit of respite to us learners simmering in the classroom. I wonder if it is possible to cook a boy in a classroom, if you could keep the sun at the correct angle, beaming straight in through a window into his eyes as it is presently. Or maybe you could just cook his eyeballs. The thought of eyeballs takes me back to the tale of the Hag and her enjoyment of that particular delicacy.

Helen described her eating them like quail's eggs, popping them in whole and then breaking the harder outer rim with her gums to get to the juicy innards. I nearly laugh, but stop myself. Something that always strikes me about laughter: the laughter of others is communal, they are all doing it, and all about the same thing. My laughter is private, about things in my head that would need explaining to non-comprehending people who don't see the joke. I imagine how the conversation would go.

'What are you laughing at?'

'The way the Hag in the Woods eats children's eyeballs.'

No, that would not help on the 'trying to not get bullied' front. The Hag in the Woods is a story that would be familiar to most of the children in this room. If their parents hadn't told it to them, they would have found out about it from friends, books or news articles about the wood that mentioned the famous local legend. They would at least have an inkling of what it was about. The difference is that I'm increasingly thinking it's real. I shake my head, a tinier movement than last time, which I manage to conceal better so there is no laughter, and try to focus on the algebra in front of me.

I'm lost, and if I were any of the other pupils I would put my hand up and ask for help, but my hands stay like leaden weights on the desk in front of me.

Chapter Eight

The trip to the woods on Saturday never happens in the end. One of Helen's friends calls, my Auntie Vera (not a biological Auntie, but one I adopted on account of her being an Auntie-like family friend. They are usually the best kind of Auntie, the ones you choose). Vera is going to look at a new house in town, downsizing now that her children have left home and her husband has died, leaving her knocking around in a large three-bedroomed semi on her own, and needs a friend to go with to act as a second pair of eyes and for the support. They turn the event into a full day out as they haven't seen enough of each other lately, so have lunch and do a bit of shopping.

At first I'm relieved that Helen won't be coming, but as the day gets nearer I'm more and more nervous about going back to the woods on my own. This uneasiness grows in my gut, and when particularly bad shivers up into my throat, making me stutter when I try to speak. The stutter is an old affliction rearing its head from when I was small. I had speech therapy to help me, only for a few weeks, and by now it's well under control, so the return of it, even if temporary, is distressing. I can remember the exercises I was taught. They are not too dissimilar to the breathing techniques Helen and I used to do together when I got upset about something, but I don't want to have to start using those any more than I do anyway.

No one from the family goes to the wood that weekend. I spend Saturday alone in the house reading, making occasional half-hearted attempts at homework, and watching the world go by out of my bedroom window. I'm happy like this, although most of the other children at school would yawn at how boring it sounds. I'm having such a nice day, I'm a little disappointed when Helen returns bearing many carrier bags.

*

The following Tuesday evening I'm in my room sitting on the floor, back resting against the bed, re-watching Star Wars, when the telephone rings and

Helen goes to answer it.

I'm not listening to what she's saying, but after a short pause she calls up the stairs in a questioning tone that the call is for me and it's someone from school. She sounds bemused, as am I. At first I think maybe one of the bullies has found my telephone number to continue the torment from the comfort of their own home out of school time, but that's silly. By now, I'm half-way down the stairs and reaching my hand out for the receiver Helen's offering. She shrugs as she goes back into the living room. Tentatively, I speak into the receiver.

'Hello?'

'Tom?' A woman's voice.

'Ye-es?' I'm wary.

'Tom, it's Sue Roberts from the library at school!'

I am silent. Sue tries again.

'You know, the librarian! You were in the library the other day, well you are most days aren't you? Haha! And you asked me about physics and shadows and...'

'Oh!' I interrupt. 'Oh, yes, sorry, it's weird hearing a teacher using their first name.'

'Oh, ho ho yes, so sorry, it must seem a bit odd.' Sue Roberts sounds flighty and nervous, which puts me a little at ease. At least I'm not the only one having anxiety here.

'It's just you reminded me of something.' Her voice lowers a notch, conspiratorial, as though someone has entered the room and she doesn't want them to hear. 'You asked me about the legend of the Hag in the Woods, and then about shadows. Please feel free to tell me to get lost, I mean who wants to be seen out and about with a teacher or someone from the school?' She's jabbering. I get the impression she wants this conversation over with as much as I do. 'But I wondered if you'd like to meet up sometime for a coffee or something to discuss it all? I know how mad it sounds. But I have more information that I think you might like, or find useful, or something. I didn't remember until after you'd left the library that day. Something about you asking for the Hag story and then mentioning shadows, and it's all come back to me. I mean I'm not sure why you were asking or if you were really that interested or only killing time but...'

'Yes, okay.' I feel like the composed, grown up one.

'Sorry dear?'

'Yes, we can meet up to talk about all that. When

would you like to?' I'm a super-efficient business person arranging a brainstorming session, or whatever it is business people do.

'Oh! Oh, that would be marvellous, thank you so much. Um, shall we say Saturday coming up then? I could pick you up or - no, that might be weird. Um, you could meet me in town maybe? I know a nice little place, they do fantastic cakes, my treat of course, and we can have a good old natter.' She sounds so relieved I almost laugh at her.

'Yes, that would be fine. I'll be on the bus, so meet you in the station? About 11?'

'Perfect!' Her voice sings down the line, triumphant.

'Right, see you Saturday then,' I say, only now aware of the gravity of what I'm agreeing to. I'm too intrigued to pass up a chance of more information on the Hag though, and if I have to meet the exuberant library lady on a day when I'd rather be in my room reading, then so be it. I hang up and go back upstairs.

*

I'm up early on Saturday to be sure of catching the right bus to meet up with Sue (as she insists I call her). By this point I no longer care much if anyone from the school sees us, even though I have agonised about that ever since getting off the phone with her. An idea which might have been mortifying a few weeks ago now seems quite normal. I want to hear whatever she might say today, and if anybody sees us and asks what we are up to I'll simply tell them the truth, which will be far more boring that whatever they might have been imagining, most likely. They will laugh, and walk away, and that will be that.

I almost don't recognise Sue hovering by the benches in the bus station. She is wearing jeans for a start, which I've never seen her in before, and a bright red jumper. Gone is the long skirt and brilliant white blouse that make up her school uniform. She looks relaxed and, well, normal. Teachers do not usually look normal. Stepping off the bus, hoping I haven't picked up any of the cloying damp smell that pervades its every surface, I head in her direction. Now that I'm here, the day's taken on a surreal edge, like a dream.

From Wednesday until today, I haven't been to the library on any of my breaks. The thought of going there and having any further conversation with Sue (I'll never get used to calling her that) is far too uncomfortable a notion. And now we're on speaking terms I can't slip in unnoticed and occupy my desk in the corner without saying anything. Everything has changed. She looked up my telephone number on the class register, or wherever it is held, and phoned me and arranged to meet. This is an unprecedented situation and one I'm not sure how to handle, except for to do what I always do; go along with it and see what happens, like a passive observer and not someone who is directly involved. It's a coping strategy that's got me through many difficulties, including the deaths of my parents, which I've only in recent years begun to think of as something that happened to me and not to some other poor child.

Sue beams at me. She is one of the more easy-to-like adults associated with the school, not officially being a teacher and only inhabiting the one room most of the time, and that being a room entered voluntarily, unlike the other classrooms. She doesn't cause any trouble for the pupils, handing out detentions and homework like the teachers do. As I reach her she claps her hands together once, as though congratulating me for getting this far across that expanse of tarmac.

'Hello, Tom!'

I endure an attack of shyness, muttering, 'Alright,' bobbing my head in acknowledgement. I've seen older boys greeting each other like this and it looks so cool, I wanted try it out. I vow never to do it again. I smile broadly instead, blustering, 'Sorry, I mean hello,' and laugh at myself.

Sue chats easily as we walk along together, one topic flowing into another without any need for my input. In the school library her personality is hidden behind the books and the silence, but here, in a social context, I find her warm and engaging, if a little too talkative for me. Today, I'm glad of that though, as it saves me from having to think of anything to say. I only have to nod, or 'Hmm,' every so often to show I'm listening. Later on that day, I wouldn't be able to tell you any of the things that Sue told me on our short walk to the café, although I could tell you that she was able to pack an extraordinary number of words into that five minute space.

My habit of trying to think of something to say all the time is too strong, however, and it carries on in my head, despite it being clear that she doesn't need me to say anything. Oh, I could mention... or maybe bring up... but, oh, the subject's changed. I saunter along next to her, trying to quieten my internal monologue, which threatens to drown her voice out at times.

The café is a small bistro nestled on a corner in a residential part of town, away from the main shopping area. Condensation clings to the windows. We go in, the door making a faraway *bing-bong* noise as we pass through. I gravitate to the table in the window, furthest away from the counter, and sit down. We are the only people in here apart from a short woman behind the counter who greets Sue like an old friend, coming around the counter to hug her. When she lets go, Sue flicks her hair about, patting at it.

'What would you like to drink?' she calls.

'Cappuccino, please.' Might as well have a treat.

She returns a couple of minutes later with a cappuccino and a huge slice of chocolate cake on a purple plate, which she puts in front of me. She only has a drink. I thank her profusely - chocolate cake is my favourite - and momentarily forget the purpose of our meeting as I grab my fork and dig in. I put too much of the delicious gooey stuff in my mouth and struggle to chew it, hoping Sue doesn't notice my bulging cheeks. She takes two delicate sips of her coffee.

'So Tom, I'm sorry to call you out here on a Saturday, you probably had football or something you'd much rather do instead.' I shake my head, unable to speak around the mouthful of food. Sue smiles. 'It's just, as I said on the phone, I was reminded about something. When you asked about the Hag story and then you mentioned shadows. I didn't make the connection straight away, but that night I was thinking and it all sort of fell into place. I had to ring you or try to catch you at school. I think... Well, let me tell you what I have to tell you and then you can tell me what you think, eh?' The solid block of cake in my mouth has shrunk by a small amount. I manage a grunt of consent.

'I must have been about your age, or not much older anyway. That's why I didn't remember straight away. It was a long time ago!' She laughs, her nerves showing in the raised pitch, but is soon serious again, cradling her coffee and watching me chew. 'I wasn't very popular at school and wasn't having a very nice time. I mean, it's awful really, isn't it? Growing up? Ghastly.' She looks down into her coffee, swirling it between her hands, and then back up to me. 'Well, anyway, I would always be on my own walking to and from school, nobody ever wanted to walk with me, and to be honest I didn't really want them to. So really, I wasn't too different from you, but that doesn't matter anyway.' She dismisses the notion with her hand, waving it away like a lazy fly hanging around the sugar bowl.

I feel the weight of unwanted attention on me. Of course she's noticed I'm a loner. It's not normal to spend all your lunch breaks in the school library when all the other children are outside doing whatever it is they do all the time. It's obvious I have no friends.

I finish the first mouthful of cake with a gulp, and plunge in again with my fork, going for a smaller portion this time. My neck's getting hot and I hope she moves onto the tale of the Hag, or whatever she has to tell me, soon. Sue is quiet for a few moments, drinking her coffee, and my eyes roam from her to take in more of my surroundings. This café is one of those little places that everybody is familiar with and walks passed dozens of times, but rarely ventures into. The sort of place it's hard to see how they make a living, as they always seem to be empty. Inside, it's homely and compact. It's more like sitting in somebody's front room than in a commercial establishment, and I like that. This despite the plastic table cloths the colour of tomato sauce, and the framed posters on the walls depicting the various places the owners have been on their holidays over the years; Majorca, Benidorm, Crete. Running a café must be more lucrative than it looks, unless they haven't been to these places but only put the posters up to lend the place a more glamorous air. I realise that Sue is talking, and tear my gaze from the bright turquoise sea in the Crete poster, looking back to her. She is in full flow.

'I knew about the story of the Hag, of course. Everybody did, much like today. My parents tried to threaten me with her if I wasn't doing what they wanted, but what I never told them was that it didn't scare me all that much. I knew it was only a story. Probably there had been some poor lonely old woman living out there once, and people made up stories about her, in that nasty gossipy way people do about someone who's a bit different, and the stories just hadn't died when she did.

'But the shadows were something else, and they did

scare me, in the end at least. I'm not sure if they're the same things that you meant when you asked about shadows in the library the other day - maybe you really did want a book about physics.' She gives me a knowing look, and then smiles when I do. 'But I'll just tell you what happened to me, and then it's up to you if it's useful or not, isn't it? You can listen, and then decide whether it's any good to you, or whether I'm just a daft old bat making things up!' She drains her mug, but keeps hold of it with both hands, resting on the table. I do the same, pushing the chocolate-stained plate aside so I can get hold of my mug properly. It's still slightly warm despite being empty, and provides an anchor point.

'I was at school in the week, obviously, and doing things with my parents at the weekends, trundling along, same old routine, nothing interesting, and then, gradually, at around your age, I noticed shadows that were just... off somehow.' She waves a hand vaguely and then lets it rest against her mug again. 'There was a cat, and other small animals, and others that weren't distinct shapes so I couldn't tell what they were. Only one or two at first, and then more and more as the next few weeks went on. I saw them all the time. It didn't matter if there was no sun or anything. And they moved in a funny way.'

'Yes, just like that.' My voice is thick and heavy. Sue gives a small nod, her mouth tight.

'I wasn't alarmed or scared, but simply intrigued. They were never in the right places, they didn't appear at the right times of day, and they didn't need any light to exist. Fascinating, really. They were in the house, in the bedroom I shared with my sister, although I'm sure she couldn't see them. She would have said. I never asked her though.

'It's going to sound daft, but I thought the shadows were mine. They kept me company. Friendly things, sort of familiars I suppose, you know how suspicious children can be,' she looks down at her cup, 'I fancied myself as a magical witch and these were my servants or some nonsense like that - some silly notion I had. Silly girl.' She shakes her head, a pinkish blush appearing on her cheeks. I want to say, 'I thought they were mine too!' and try to alleviate the pressure on her, but my mouth won't open.

'After a little while, they came with me wherever I

went, following, and sometimes going on ahead and kind of leading the way. I've no clue how, but they knew where I wanted to go and went on before me a lot of the time.

'The Old Wood was a lot more popular then; everybody went there. I grew up in Annisthorpe, just like you. Lovely place. We moved here when I was in my late teens and it took me so long to get used to all the noises and goings-on in a town after only being used to a place that fell asleep at eight every night. I couldn't sleep properly for weeks. Little things like people walking past on the street would keep me awake.

'Anyway, Annisthorpe was thick with gossip about the Hag then, mainly because people were terrified of their children climbing that massive beech tree that used to be there and falling out. I think the old story was more popular then, you don't hear so much about it nowadays. Presumably because nobody really goes in the wood anymore, do they?'

'Not much.'

'Parents knew the games children played, egging each other on to go higher and higher, and the winds around here, Tom, especially when you get out of the town and the shelter of all the buildings, they can gust ever so suddenly. So the fear was that, even if a child was a really good climber, they might be taken by one of those sudden gusts of wind and come a cropper.' She tries to take another sip of coffee but her mug is empty and she puts it back down with a forlorn expression. She sighs.

'Anyway, I would often cut through the Wood to get to a friends house. Yes, I did manage to have a couple of friends, off and on. So, after the shadows came, I continued doing this, seeing no reason to change, and I felt like they really liked it in the Old Wood. It was like taking a dog for a walk, when you get to their favourite park and you can sense their happiness. In the wood the shadows would become agitated, and swarm in a way that they didn't anywhere else. And they always wanted to get me off the path. It sounds crazy, doesn't it?

'The way to my friend's house was straight across the wood and out the other side. You didn't need to go anywhere near the giant beech, although you could see it of course, over to the side of you as you went past. There was no missing that thing. But, no matter which way I was going, to my friend's or back again, the shadows always started swarming in the direction of the tree, and I really felt like they were trying to pull me in that direction.

'It didn't hold any fear for me. As I said, I thought the story of the Hag was just that: a fairy tale for people to scare each other with, and I wasn't a tree climber. I was a rather dumpy, unathletic girl, so I knew I wouldn't be the slightest bit tempted to try and climb a tree like that. I wouldn't even attempt the apple tree in our garden, although my sister was always up it. Would you like something else? Another drink?'

'No thanks.' I want her to get on with the rest of the story.

'Okay.' A tense smile. 'One day I had more time than usual because my friend and I were bored, so I left early to go home. I was dawdling along, killing time. The shadows were there, as always. I was so used to them by then I would have been quite freaked out if they didn't show up. When we got to the part of the wood with the giant beech in they did their usual flocking around me, getting terribly excited, all climbing over one another, moving fast, trying to lead me to it. I was at a loose end, I didn't need to be home for a good half an hour or so, so couldn't see any harm in having a wander around the woods for a while. I followed them.

'The wood was more densely knitted in those days. That beech wasn't the only tree they cut down. There were a few other smaller ones that went before it too. The shadows picked out a path between all the tree trunks, navigating the thick brambles sticking out everywhere and the nettles nearly as tall as me.

'It was autumn, leaves everywhere, every different sort you could think of. I kicked them up as I walked, watching them scattering and landing in the nettles. It was quite a windy day too, as I recall. The shadows were very agitated, shifting about, growing and getting smaller again, but quicker than usual. Does that sound familiar?'

I nod, resisting the urge to blurt out 'I saw it too! The body!' I keep the words inside my mouth, like that chocolate cake, not letting Sue see.

'Hmm,' she nods, taking a deep breath. 'There's no easy way to say the next part so I'll just get on with it. They led me to the base of the giant beech, and there was a body there,' she swallows. 'A dead body. A female one.'

My eyes widen as she says the words I hadn't dared to hope she would. But as they're ringing in my ears, I'm thinking that this was over forty years ago, surely. Mrs Roberts is close to retirement age. It must have been a different body. I daren't speak, worried about sounding foolish, whatever I say. It must be a coincidence. Two people had met their end at the base of the tree, in the space of forty-odd years.

'You saw a body too, didn't you?' I wish I was as brave as her, to come out with it like that. I nod. 'The same body.' Not a question. I look away from her to the far end of the café where the small woman who greeted her so enthusiastically is busying herself with cups and saucers, disappearing into a room in the back, and reappearing every few minutes, her neat dark hair bobbing with her activities.

'How did you know?' My voice sounds tiny, and I daren't look back at Sue. Not yet.

'I didn't really, but I thought I would ask. It was the same body.' Sue gets up, goes over to the woman I'm watching, and orders more drinks. She doesn't ask if I want one, but comes back with another massive cappuccino to put in front of me. I'm so grateful to have a fresh warm cup to put my hands around I could hug her, and smile despite myself.

'Thanks!'

'We need hot drinks while we're talking about this stuff.'

I take a too-soon gulp and it burns my throat. I wipe the froth moustache off before Sue notices. My breathing has been getting shallower the more Sue talks, but I didn't notice until now. I want to avoid having to perform my breathing techniques in front of Sue, even though she would in all likelihood only smile and be totally understanding about it. We are quiet, each not looking at the other. I take another, more careful, sip of my drink for courage.

'I saw her, but she wasn't on the tape.'

'Wasn't on the tape?' I have her full attention, and that creeping warmth returns to my neck.

'Yes. Erm, I have an old second-hand video camera I took to the woods with me. Just messing about, you know. Wanted to do a bit of filming of the trees and stuff. When I saw the body I filmed that too, but when I watched the tape back there was nothing there.' I don't mention how many times I watched the tape.

'Oh, I see. Gosh. And the tape was blank?' Her eyes don't leave my face for a second and I feel like that blush I hate so much must be making my spots flare like beacons. I stare at the froth clinging to the inside of my cup.

'No. It had recorded, but the body wasn't there.' I take in a glut of air, close my mouth, blink, and let out a long controlled breath, pretending I'm blowing on my drink to cool it down. She's not fooled. My face is too hot, but I plough on.

'I was filming, looking through the viewfinder at the body. It was there, unmistakeable. It started to rain so I ran home, but when I watched the tape the body had gone, and all the leaves and everything.' I sigh, looking up at Sue, relieved to get it out. I hope she'll interrupt, but she only sits, close-mouthed, eyes searching my face. I look away, taking in another deep breath.

'When I saw the body, straight away the shadows went off somewhere. I've not seen them at all since. I didn't notice at first because I was looking at the body. It was... I didn't touch it, but I couldn't take my eyes off it, and I was dreading having to tell somebody, and what might happen after that. A big investigation, the police, the neighbours all talking about it and knowing I was the one who'd discovered it. I think I was more scared by that than the actual body. The body couldn't do me any harm.' I gaze at the clear shining water in the Crete poster. It calms me a little. Places that look like that exist in the world, so dream-like and improbable, so why couldn't a body that's there one minute, gone the next? The colour of that sea is mesmerising.

'She had one arm cocked up against the tree, suspended,' I put my arm up in imitation, glancing at Sue for a sign of recognition. Her face is blank. 'She looked like she was waving. "Not Waving but Drowning." Do you know that poem? I really like it. Anyway,' My arm drops back to the table between us. 'What did she look like to you?'

'The same. "Not Waving but Drowning." Exactly that.'

My biggest feeling on discovering the body was one of panic at the thought of all the chaos and movement that usually follows such a discovery, and me right at the centre of it. I hadn't been able to admit that to myself until now, as it made me feel even more of a coward. My strongest reaction when I saw that the body had disappeared on the tape was one of enormous relief, and the reason I watched it over and over was to check it hadn't reappeared. With no evidence that I ever saw it, only the images inside my own head, I felt a powerful lack of obligation to do anything about it.

'I wonder if she's still there.' I didn't mean to say it out loud. The words dazzle me, hanging in the air between us.

'No, I think she's a ghost. I've had almost forty years to think about this, and I've been back to the wood countless times too. Not recently, but I used to call in every now and then. Not sure why, really. I never saw anything more unusual than the occasional bastard hacking a tree down with a chainsaw.' Hearing her swear is thrilling. 'I think the shadows wanted me to see her, for what reason I have no idea. After I had seen the body, I never saw those shadows ever again, to this day. Have you seen them again?'

'No.' I'm disappointed I have nothing more to tell her. She nods.

'What really puzzles me, shadows aside, is who was she? I've checked back through old editions of the local paper as far as I can, but can't find anything about the discovery of the body of a woman or girl underneath a giant beech tree in the Old Wood. Something like that would warrant a mention, surely. Was she murdered? Did she fall out of the tree? Who was she? There's simply nothing, a complete blank, when you start to research it. It's as though she never existed. Yet, there she was. And forty years later, there she was again.'

That's enough, I reach my limit. My breathing is shallow, and the café walls move like the shadows on the edge of my vision. I try to focus on my coffee cup, empty except for streaks of brown froth up the sides. My capacity for stressful conversation and intriguing information has been reached, I can process no more. I stand up too fast, knocking my chair into the wall behind me, and take one step to the side, hanging on the table.

'Sorry, I just...' and before I know what's happening I'm outside in the crisp air, Mrs Roberts holding me steady by the elbow, performing my breathing exercises without thinking about it.

'Sorry,' I blurt between gasps. My face is burning from embarrassment and the effort of getting my breathing under control. I try not to lean on Sue or get too close to her, but can't stand on my own yet. From what I can see of her face, when I'm not staring straight at the ground in front of my feet, Sue looks devastated, and it dawns on me she might think she's caused this. I can't get enough breath to explain to her.

'Not at all. Let's get you home, come on.' She's pushing at my elbow.

All I can say is sorry - a nice short word, easy to sigh out - over and over, as Sue, stricken, leads me away from the café. She natters about anything and everything - it must be a nervous response - as we make our way through the streets back to the bus station, my elbow propped in her hand. It's slow going. She talks on all manner of subjects, but noticeably avoids anything to do with the Old Wood and whatever is or isn't there.

Sue walks at an angle, half in front of me, like she's trying to shield me from the gaze of passers by. She chatters on about the weather, school stuff, what's for dinner tonight, and what she might like to catch on the television over the weekend. I wonder if she could stop if she wanted to. My breathing is better, much calmer than before, and I look up from the pavement more often. Sue is such a chatterbox, it makes me wonder how she can stand the silence of the library all day every day.

It's forty-five minutes before the next bus leaves for Annisthorpe. I hope Sue will leave me alone in the station and go home, or go to do some shopping, but she's too concerned and says she can't go until she's sure I'm okay.

We sit on the bench we met at this morning. Sue tells me my colour is returning to normal, and I can feel my skin is cooler.

'Sorry,' I say once more, an incongruous laugh escaping at the absurdity of the situation, and how many times I've said that word in the past few minutes.

'Does that happen often?'

'Not as often as it used to, and I handle it better than I used to, believe it or not. I hate it.' I scrunch my brow up, until I take one last big breath and my face relaxes.

'I'm sorry too. This was probably a bad idea.'

'No, I'm glad I came. It's feels great that I'm not the only one to have seen the body, even if it does make everything more confusing.'

We sit in silence, listening to the buses roaring

around the station, watching the endless stream of people coming and going, always in a rush regardless of direction. A place like this represents everything I hate: the noise, the concrete, the disregard for nature or anything pleasant. I pity the pigeons that flutter down to the tarmac for crumbs, flying away at the last second when a bus approaches. There must be somewhere better they could live than a bus station.

I remember something then. 'We never got to talk about the Hag.'

Sue looks at me unblinking, eyes faraway, and gives the tiniest of nods, apparently having made up her mind about something.

'Come to the library on one of your lunch breaks next week if you can. I've got something that might be of interest.'

Chapter Nine

I get home earlier than I expect with no further incidents. It feels like I've been out all day, but it's not yet four o'clock when I walk through the door. I've had time to process things better on the half hour journey home and I'm glad I went, despite all the awkwardness and embarrassment. I should be used to awkwardness and embarrassment being a normal part of my life anyway.

I tick off the main points over and over, no longer trying to make sense of them. The same body, in the same position, but forty years apart. Apparently, too, the same shadows. A lonely, isolated girl, and a lonely, isolated boy, both around fourteen years of age. Body there one minute, and gone the next, forever, or until the next fourteen year old child who can see the shadows and can't resist following them comes along.

In an attempt to stop it from going around in my head, I grab a new exercise book from the drawer and sketch out the main points. I write 'Old Wood' in large bubble letters on the cover and keep it aside for any future notes I might want to make, sliding it into the top of another drawer, where there is just room for it on top of all the bits of paper, books and general bric-a-brac in there, before heading down for dinner.

*

I don't want to speak to Mrs Roberts too soon, so instead of rushing to the library the first chance I get on Monday, I leave it for a couple of days. I don't want to look too eager, and also don't want to fill my head with too much information in too short a space of time.

On the days I don't go to the library, I usually go to a particular corner of the playing field. This is my corner, regardless of how many other children might also think it's theirs. On the days I'm there none of the other children want to be there, so I always get it to myself. It's a nice little nook behind the drooping willow tree, with a rough wooden bench, nothing more than a plank on legs. I quite often get a book out and read while eating my lunch. A good book and a peanut butter sandwich is my idea of heaven.

Wednesday is rainy and I think I've left enough time after the excitement of Saturday to be able to face Mrs Roberts again. I'm intrigued and at the same time dreading being shown something else that might only confuse everything further.

I climb the stairs up to the school library, going the opposite way to all the other pupils, who are streaming down like a waterfall, doubling back on themselves with the staircase's hairpin bends on their way down to the gym, where tables are set out for them to eat their lunch at, or some of them will be heading home to have their lunch there. I squash myself against the bannister when the torrent of pupils coming the other way threatens to knock me off my feet, and then take the last flight, where there are no other pupils left, two steps at a time. It's a rare display of athleticism I would never risk if anyone was there to see it. If someone was watching I'd be bound to slip and break my nose, or perform some other humiliating feat of clumsiness.

I pause before entering the library to check my breathing has returned to normal after my climb up the stairs.

Mrs Roberts is sitting where she always does, at her desk half-way across the same wall the door is on, reading. I don't mess about pretending to be interested in the books this time, instead going straight up to her and standing in front of her desk until she notices me. She looks surprised to see me, which sets off a big wheel of doubt in my mind. Maybe she's forgotten what she said on Saturday, or didn't mean it. Maybe I'm going mad and none of it ever happened. Or maybe it was only that she was so engrossed in her book, anybody suddenly standing in front of her would have elicited that response. At least, that's what she tells me.

'I should've expected to see you today,' she smiles, waving towards the window, which is getting pelted with rain.

'Yes,' is all I can think of to say.

'Just wait here a moment, if that's okay. It's in my bag.' She gets up and disappears into the depths of the library. For want of anything else to do, I stand motionless and wait. She's taking a long time. I imagine her finding a secret door to the stairwell and making her escape, having not wanted to see me after all, or forgetting about me and going for her tea break. I think about getting a book down to look at, but don't seem to be able to move. After a few minutes have passed, I sit on a chair at the desk closest to Mrs Roberts' and continue waiting.

She emerges holding a fat brown envelope, her expression distracted, and her skin puffy and blotched under her eyes.

'So sorry,' she's saying as she returns to her desk, not noticing where I'm sitting. I get up and stand in front of her again. 'Sorry, I didn't mean to take so long. It's a big thing for me, showing you this. I mean, giving you this! I don't need it for goodness sake!' I'm lost.

'I've never shown another living soul, you see. Sorry. There's something I didn't tell you on Saturday, and sorry again for that, by the way,' I'm thinking that's nearly as many apologies as I gave her on Saturday. She shakes her head, waving the envelope to the side, as if irritated at herself. When she smiles up at me, it looks fake.

'Do sit down, please.'

We are the only people in the library. I go back to the chair I was sitting on a moment before, and pull it up to her desk to sit opposite her. A thought pops into my mind that this must be how a job interview feels, or a police interview. Some sort of interview, anyway.

Sue clutches the envelope, holding it up between us, as though the mere sight of it should mean something to me.

'Yes, sorry, there's something I didn't tell you on Saturday. On that day, when I was early walking home, remember, and I saw the body, I also saw something else.' She puts the envelope down on the desk between us with a sigh.

'You're familiar with the tale of the Hag in the Woods, obviously. Well, that day all those years ago, when I was an impressionable young girl, after the shadows had long gone, I lingered to look at the body for possibly longer than I should have. You had that feeling, I'm sure. I didn't want to turn away, it felt disrespectful, and she was so pale but felt like she'd been alive only moments before. Do you see what I mean?' I nod, mouth shut tight.

'Hmm. I stayed for longer than I should have I think, and after a little while I got this awful feeling that I was not alone. They say the Hag lives, or used to live, in a bower the other side of the ridge near to where the giant beech is. Well, as I say, I felt as though there was someone else there with me.' She pauses, rubbing her eyes, her fingertips moving up to her eyebrows to smooth them out.

'The other day in the café, we didn't get to the part where I left the wood. You didn't get to find out how that happened. Well, now.' She takes a deep breath. I can't take my eyes off her. 'I felt there was somebody else there while I was looking at the body, and I turned, purely on instinct, to see who it was.' She looks up straight into my eyes. I try not to flinch. 'Beyond that ridge I saw the top of a head. It had steel grey hair, dishevelled. It hadn't been washed or brushed in a long time. And there was a pair of heavy grey eyes looking right at me, unwavering. It was an old woman, a very old woman. I was young and impressionable enough, and had heard enough about the Hag in the Woods to convince myself that this was her glaring at me.' I'm unable to hold eye contact any longer, and look down at the desk. This must be the first time she's told anyone this.

'Tom, I ran. I ran faster than I had ever run before, or have since. I ran until I couldn't feel the ground under my feet, swerving around the trees, and I never looked back. I ran and ran until I was well clear of the giant beech and the gates to the Old Wood, and I kept on running until I was home.

'I daren't tell my parents what I had seen, so I kept it to myself, both about the body and the old woman.

'You might think I was crazy to ever go back, but I had to check, you see. I had to see if the body was still there. I knew if there really was a body lying there in the woods, something would have to be done about it. You knew that too. I should think you were very relieved when you saw the tape was blank. I would have been.' I bite my tongue, resisting the urge to correct her. The tape wasn't blank, I want to say, everything was still there, only the body and the leaves were missing. And I don't want to talk about how relieved I was that the body didn't show up.

'So a couple of days later, when I was due to go to my friend's house again, I went through the woods. I hadn't seen the shadows since that day at the giant beech. I felt sure I would never see them again, and indeed, I haven't. Well, you know what I'm going to say, don't you? Yes, that time there was no sign of the body.

I walked to my friend's house, relieved and confused.'

She opens the envelope and lets the contents fall onto the table between us. Dozens and dozens of newspaper clippings, fusty and old, and some barely held together along the crease lines where they have been folded for decades, cascade over her desk. Most of them are small scraps, a photograph, or a paragraph clipped from a page buried deep in the bowels of a newspaper tens of years before. Straight away I can see what they are. Sue had researched the Hag, with the same sort of obsessive fire that I have when I'm studying something, and these clippings were the result.

'In the next few weeks after the incident in the wood, and before it became so far away in my memory that I forgot the details, I got as many copies of as many different local papers as I could get my hands on. Some I bought, most I begged from friends or relatives after they'd finished with them. My parents assumed I was studying how to be a journalist, but what I was actually doing was scouring them tirelessly, for hours on end, for titbits of information about the Hag in the Woods.'

She picks up two of the clippings and lets them fall through her fingers back to the desk.

'I didn't find any articles that were actually about her, but she is mentioned here and there in passing, hovering around the edges of other stories, in the shadows, always lurking, never stepping into the light. There's no mention at all of a body, as I said.' She's looking at me, but her eyes are far away.

'I did this for a few weeks, but eventually stopped because it was so futile. I haven't opened this envelope for so many years. I don't even know why I kept it. But now that we've had our little chat, I think I'd like you to have it, if you want it. I think you're at the same stage that I was all those years ago, looking for something to make sense of it all, so this can be my tiny way of helping with that. Maybe you'll find something in all this that I missed.

'The Hag is only ever mentioned in a vague way in any of them, and there is the occasional 'artist's impression' of her too, which might amuse you.

'Anyway, here you are, if you want them.' She pushes them across the desk towards me but I daren't reach out to touch them yet. It feels wrong to take something that's been kept for so long by someone else. They are obviously important to her.

'Go on!' she says with a little laugh, but her eyes are glistening. 'You have far more need of them than I do, or you wouldn't have come in here the other week asking about the Hag. I really hope you can glean more from them than I ever did.' She's drawing them back to her, sweeping them with her arm to the edge of the desk. She stuffs them back into the envelope, almost carelessly, as though she can't wait to be rid of them, and hands it to me.

*

Old, sepia bits of paper. I'm sitting cross-legged on my bed with the clippings in a small heap before me, like the embers of a fire. I rub one lightly between a thumb and forefinger; it's like fabric. It has a drape. It has textures and fibres in it. Tiny dots of ink accumulate and spread to form an image. I let the cutting drop to land on the pile with the others. They are like confetti, or leaves fallen from a tree. They are soft and saggy in that way that only very old paper can be when it doesn't go stiff like a board. I wonder what makes the difference. I spend several minutes here gazing at them, lifting them and letting them drift down, enjoying the sensual nature of the paper with its frayed edges and silken grain.

As Mrs Roberts warned me, there isn't much new information in these clippings, but I appreciate them more for their own history in that fusty envelope which they have lived in for the best part of forty years, than for any enlightenment they might offer regarding the Hag.

For the main part, they repeat the same information in different ways. There was said to be a Hag who lived in a bower at the edge of the wood. Some called her Annis (that is new, I didn't know that. So that's how the village got its name). One of the clippings calls her Black Annis, because of the peculiar hue of her skin. Descriptions of her range from presenting a dotty but generally normal old lady to a sort of troll or ogre character whose footsteps have shaped the very ground we walk on. The only agreement the authors of all these clippings can reach is that she was old, female and lived in the woods somewhere close to a giant beech tree, all of which I already know. She was either to be feared or pitied, or both.

I flop back onto the bed, keeping my legs crossed, my head hitting the pillow perfectly, making me smile.

I'm formulating a plan. It's a simple plan, and one I shall execute alone.

I'm going back to the woods and I'm going to walk straight through them. If there are any shadows, I will ignore them. I will go right up to the stump of the old giant beech tree and push on to the ridge beyond where the bower or cave, or whatever is there, waits. If there is anything under the tree stump that should not be there I won't let it distract me. I'll simply go straight to that ridge and see what lies beyond. Or whom.

Chapter Ten

It's weeks until I get to put my plan into action. I've seen nothing more of the shadows in this time, as I expected, and I've hardly gone to the school library either. I did go a couple of times soon after the day Mrs Roberts gave me the clippings, and she did what she always does - sat at her desk, reading until disturbed - but it's too awkward being in the same space as her now that we have shared secrets. I have her clippings, which she guarded for years, never showing to anyone. She knows I've seen the body.

I'm spending more time in the corner of the playing field, and I go home to have a bite to eat there sometimes. It's too far really, and only gives me about fifteen minutes to sit down and eat something before I have to set off back to school again, but I relish the idea of escaping from school in the daytime. I get to feel like a rebel, which I am anything but.

I'm careful to only go home for my lunch on days when Helen and Bob won't be in. I can pretend to be grown up, letting myself in with my key and enjoying having the house to myself for a few minutes. I find I'm able, for ten or fifteen minutes, to quieten down my mind, focusing on the task of making a sandwich, getting a plate, carrying it through to the living room, sitting in Granddad's armchair (a special treat, that), and simply being me for a while with no obligation to act a certain way for anyone else. I heave a huge sigh when it's time to get up again, take the plate back through to the kitchen, rinse it, dry it, put it away, and make my way back to school, wondering if I somehow look different having been out and about rather than incarcerated in the walls and fences there.

The surprising part about my plan is that it ends up involving someone other than me, and possibly the Hag. It happens in one of those self-conscious blurs that occur when someone like me, who is used to their own company, unexpectedly finds themselves talking to, and actually enjoying the conversation with, another person they appear to have things in common with.

She's sitting in my corner of the playing field when I saunter over, lost in a daydream so I don't notice her until I'm right in front of her.

I was looking forward to reading my book while I ate my sandwiches, but it never leaves my bag. She won't move. For some reason, this girl has planted herself on my bench and looks like she plans to stay there all day. My mind is a whirlpool wanting to know who this is and how I can get her to go away without being rude. I've never noticed her before. She's not in school uniform like the rest of us, instead sitting on my bench in jeans and a t-shirt as if that's a normal thing to do. All I want is my bench back, and to read my book.

I notice her hair. It's a pale blonde, almost white, and looks soft. I have no intention of touching it to see if it feels as soft as it looks. By the time I notice her it's too late to turn back and walk away. That would look weird. So I perch awkwardly on the opposite end of the bench, as far away from her as I can get, resigning myself to an excruciating hour of trying to enjoy my sandwiches without making any eating sounds, and not being able to read my book. I stare at my lunch, out at the field, over to my right as if fascinated by the hedge growing there - anywhere except in her direction. I try my best to pretend she's not there.

The next day, she's there again. She's not in any hurry to let me have my bench back. As I'm lifting today's sandwich to my mouth, she says, 'Hi!' as though she's only just noticed me.

Sandwich half in and half out of my mouth, I look over to her, the heat gathering under my stiff school collar. I can only grunt until I take the sandwich out of my mouth, unbitten. She laughs and says, 'I'm Claire,' and beams at me, as though this is great news and I should be very grateful.

'Hello, Claire.' I must look utterly bemused. I've never been able to hide what I'm thinking. It shows on my face for all to see. I'm clueless as to what to do next, so look at the sandwich in my hand for answers. There are none. I gulp. My hand holding the sandwich looks like a mannequin's. I can't move my neck. 'I'm Tom,' I say.

'Hi, Tom.'

We've already done 'hello', haven't we? I can't cope with this. I'm about to give up and take the massive bite I long to take out of the sandwich when Claire says,

'Are you having a good day?'

Oh god, please go away and stop talking to me. I lower the sandwich and make myself smile at her, my face stiff and uncompliant. It must be the most unconvincing smile she's ever seen. 'Not really. I'm at school'.

She laughs, slapping her leg. I must be funny, then. My face relaxes a notch and the smile feels more real, but still like it doesn't belong there. I swiftly take that bite before she can interrupt again, and chew as noisily as I like. I don't care anymore. Claire isn't eating. In fact, as I sneak another look at her as I chew, I notice she doesn't have any lunch with her, or anything else for that matter.

That lunchtime, we talk. Or, more accurately, I talk and she listens. I talk about school, and the library, and my mum and dad, my TV and VCR at home, what music I like, the folk tales I'm interested in, and my visit to the woods. The words run away from me and once I've begun talking I can't seem to stop. Claire is so attentive. Her eyes, a soft green like new moss, never leave my face and I blush furiously the entire time, but the words won't stop. I finish my lunch in between the words, chewing around them, pausing sometimes to gulp some drink. She asks one question, 'So what sort of thing do you like, Tom?' and the floodgates open. If it were anyone else, I would say they regretted asking, but Claire didn't interrupt or suddenly remember somewhere else she had to be, or look bored, or any of the other responses I'm used to on those rare occasions I speak to another person at any length. I even told her about the Hag and how interested I'd become in the story, and I might have mentioned that I think it could be real, not made up.

*

At lunchtime the next day I am sitting on the bench in the corner of the playing field with Claire again.

'Sorry for going on so much yesterday. I don't normally talk much really, it's just you seemed interested.' I've finished my sandwiches and she hasn't said much, simply sat there as if this is where she lives now, watching the other children playing on the field or sitting in groups on the grass eating and laughing, with heaps of coats and bags around them.

'I am interested! It's very interesting. I like to listen to you. I don't have any brothers or sisters so I'm used to my own company a lot.'

'Oh? Me neither. Brothers or sisters, I mean. Although, er...' I stop myself. No, that's saying too much, definitely. She looks at me curiously, but doesn't ask what I was going to say.

'It's a bit of a pain, really. It would be lovely to have someone to talk to, you know, about stuff! So much stuff to talk about and no-one there most of the time, at home anyway. Thank goodness for friends!' I don't have much idea of what she's talking about, but nod, glad to have the spotlight away from me.

'My mum and dad don't get on very well. Sorry, I don't feel like I can moan about them when you don't even have a mum and dad.'

'It's okay.'

She nods, and wrinkles her nose a little. 'Well, they're always arguing, it's horrible. I don't know when it got like that, I can't remember, but I'm sure they didn't used to argue like that all the time. Sometimes they argue about me, it's ridiculous. Me!' She shakes her head, making her hair ripple around her shoulders. 'If they'd just come up and talk to me themselves instead of staying downstairs where they think I can't hear them and talking about me, we'd probably all get on a lot better, wouldn't we?' I know nothing about warring parents, but give what I hope is an encouraging smile.

'I'm sorry, I probably shouldn't be telling you all this. You're not interested are you? It's just you told me so much and I feel like, in comparison, you hardly know anything about me, and why should you tell all that to a total stranger you know nothing about?' She laughs, flicking her hair to the side, the gap between her two front teeth showing.

Our conversations over the next few days merge into one mass in my mind like the shadows used to, overlapping and becoming indistinct from one another. I feel like I've known Claire for years. Given how much she's talking, I'm surprised she was able to stay quiet long enough for me to tell her all that I had. She's a lot like Mrs Roberts in that respect, managing to keep silent in the library all day when she must be desperate to talk, especially if stressed or worried.

I come to like Claire a great deal, not least because she appears so keen to spend time with me. When I make jokes, she laughs, which takes some getting used to. She keeps appearing on my bench over the next week or so, and our conversations flow easily. Some of the other kids notice us and call across from their football game, 'Hey, Thomas, who's your girlfriend?' making my blush burn a deeper red, but I don't pay attention to it. Claire is untroubled by them, and laughs at their taunts, seeming to enjoy the attention. She tells me she likes to dance and takes regular classes, is quite musical, but doesn't read much. The opposite to me, in fact. I never do ask her where she came from all of a sudden, or why she wears jeans every day. It doesn't seem important.

'I don't think I've ever spoken to one person so much, not even my grandparents,' I say, chuckling at how amazing it is. She smiles at me, producing dimples in her cheeks.

'Well, I'm glad. It's good to talk.' Her smile drops. 'I remember what I wanted to tell you, Tom. Since you told me about the woods and the Hag and all that, I've been having ever such funny dreams. Well, not funny. Rather horrible, in fact. I really had no idea about that story or anything. But now, I can't believe I didn't know it before, it feels like I've always known, it's sort of in my bones. It's one of those sort of stories, isn't it? Gets right under you skin.'

'Dreams?' I remember Mrs Roberts mentioned she'd dreamed about the wood, and I'd had those dreams about the shadows too.

'Yes, nearly every night since you first told me. I forgot to mention it. They disappear during the day, don't they, dreams? They're so...' She looks out into the field, holding a hand in front of her face, as though trying to hold the dream there so she can get a good look at it, '... so full of swirling shadows, dark edges everywhere. Images in leaves and trees. There's never anything concrete about them. You can't say, "Oh, this happened, and then that happened". It's just this awful sort of vortex of shadows spinning and leaves like ghosts dancing around in circles. Not like me to dream stuff like that at all. They make me dizzy. I'd quite like to visit the woods sometime.'

The delicious prospect of taking a friend to the woods with me next time I go sits in my belly like a satisfying meal.

*

The next day threatens rain and I'm not sure whether to bother going to the bench on the playing field. By the time it gets to lunch-time, there is a steady drizzle. Surely she won't be sitting there in this? I get half way across the field before I can see the bench peeking out from behind the willow tree and I'm right: she's not there.

I pause, unsure whether to go and sit there anyway and wait to see if she comes, or to find somewhere drier to go. I walk forward a few more paces, and then change my mind and turn back, trying to ignore my disappointment that she isn't there. I go back towards the building. My thoughts turn to the library, my old refuge, but Mrs Roberts will be there. Maybe I can sneak in; sidle along to my customary desk in the corner, unnoticed, and covertly eat my sandwiches there as I have done in the past, whilst looking at a book, or writing in my notepad. I opt to try that.

Most of the pupils have gone from the stairs by this time, except for a few stragglers clattering down, some taking the steps two at a time in their haste to get some food inside them. I reach the top and adjust my blazer and the bag over my shoulder, preparing for the stealthy manoeuvre I must pull off next. I suppose if she does see me I can say I don't want to talk today.

There are voices inside the library. As I get closer I recognise one as Mrs Roberts', and the other is female too. I'm fairly certain it's Claire. I stop outside the door, making myself smaller, holding my breath. My heart feels big in my chest.

'But it's unfair! I feel like I'm bullying him!' Claire is saying, 'I know you meant well, and it sounded like it would be fun. It is fun, but not in the way I thought. He's really nice, but the way we met doesn't feel right. I just wanted you to know.'

'What are you talking about, dear?' Mrs Roberts sounds agitated.

'What you asked me to do! Tom's told me the whole story about the Hag and everything, he really opened up, and I believe him.' I stop breathing when I hear my name, and hold that breath while I inch closer to the door frame to hear better. I gulp slowly, trying not to make a sound. Claire is still talking.

'... about some sort of shadows and all sorts. He thinks it's real, and I know you wanted me to convince him otherwise and put him off the idea, but, well, I've no reason not to believe him Sue, so if you thought I was going to talk some sense into him or something,

I'm not. It's dishonest, and I really like him. I won't lie to him. He's so trusting, I'm not going to tell him it's all a load of nonsense. You know it isn't anyway!'

There is silence for a second and I shift my weight delicately.

'Did you know he had some sort of panic attack after talking to me about it, Claire? He's too obsessed with it all. Real or not, it's not healthy. I only wanted to help, and I thought he would listen to someone like you more than a silly old bat like me. It was a mistake to give him those clippings. I knew that straight after I did it. What a foolish thing to do. I thought I was helping, but that's only encouraging him too, isn't it?' She sounds weary.

I can hear the exasperation in Claire's voice, 'Yes, a bit of a mixed message there, Auntie!'

I stare hard at the floor, mouth shut tight, not moving a muscle, although the temptation to scream is great. I thought I'd made a real friend. I don't want to hear any more. I move away half a step, planning to get down the stairs as fast as I can.

'I was just concerned for the boy,' I hear 'Auntie Sue' saying, and at that moment my shoe catches on the buffed surface of the landing floor, and I stumble, desperate to stay on my feet. I cast an urgent glance back through the library doorway. Claire's head whips round at the noise, and she sees me, her face aghast. I hold her gaze for one beat before legging it, as fast I can go, all the way down those hundreds of stairs. I hear a faint, 'Tom!' calling after me, but I can't tell if it's Claire or Mrs Roberts. I don't care. I want to hurl myself over the bannister and land in a jangle of bones at the bottom of the stairwell - it would be quicker - but I stagger down one by one, not brave enough to take them two at a time like some of the other boys do. I wish I could take them a flight at a time.

Outside, I can't work out what to do or where to go. There is not enough time left to get home and back in time for afternoon lessons. I'm surprised to find that I do care about getting back in time for lessons. I have a morbid fear of being late for lessons. The humiliation of walking in when all the other children are already there, staring at you. Having to stand mumbling apologies and explanations to the teacher, while your face burns like a beacon. I would rather hang around somewhere and miss the whole lesson than face that. The bench in the corner of the playing field is tainted forever. I obviously can't return to the library.

I slow my breathing and heave a sigh that comes all the way from the pit of my belly, expelling the hope of having a friend to visit the woods with. I slope to the edge of the car park, looking for an unoccupied bit of wall to sit on. I'm so hungry. A heat grows behind my eyes, threatening tears, but I swallow hard a couple of times and keep them back. All I want to do is to go home and never leave the house; hide in my room and pretend the rest of the world doesn't exist. I'd be okay, I have my TV and my books. I thought I had a friend, I think as I slump down onto the corner of a low wall surrounding some neglected bushes.

I get my sandwiches out and chew over the words I heard upstairs. They taste of hate and gossip, of manipulation and lies. I have never felt more confused or humiliated. I'm so sick of thinking about the Old Wood, the shadows, the Hag, and now I have Claire, who I can never speak to again, and 'Auntie Sue' to add to the mix, dolloping shame upon shame. It all goes round and round in my head as I chew and swallow, chew and swallow, my jaw working automatically as I stare straight ahead, avoiding eye contact with everyone around me.

By the time I finish my sandwiches and push the thin straw through the hole in the top of the apple juice carton, I've made my mind up that I must speak to someone. I've grown used to being able to talk to Claire recently. I enjoyed that so much. I gulp as more tears gather behind my eyes. I will not let them fall. Not here.

I look down into my lap, erasing the rest of the world. I won't be seeing Claire anymore, so I must find someone else to talk to about it all, and the obvious person is my grandma Helen. I have no choice, except to keep it all to myself, and I'll go mad if I do that. I had kept in the hurting after my parents died for years, and that had done me no good at all. If I learned anything, it was to talk about things, even if it was painful, uncomfortable and embarrassing. Despite knowing this I hardly ever do it, until recently with Claire. The blush returns as another wave of humiliation crashes over my head, but at the same time I resolve to speak to Helen about it. Not about Claire and Sue, but about the shadows and the Hag. She won't laugh at me or tell me I'm being silly or making a big deal out of nothing. She won't sneak around and talk about me behind my back.

I had loved the idea of Claire coming to the woods with me one day, despite understanding what we might find there. My mind had gone into overdrive, imagining seeing her outside of school, where we might meet, what we would talk about. Now, I never want to see her again. She had been drafted in as some kind of decoy friend for me to confide in. I can't comprehend what Mrs Roberts' game was, but as I relax a little and start to digest what's happened, I'm struggling to think too badly of her. She must have been trying to help in her own bizarre way, and Claire was nice, and... I shake my head to try and get rid of the thoughts spiralling around. I have no idea what to think anymore. The only person who might have an inkling of how I feel is Helen. She knows me best. I let go another big sigh, putting the lid back on my lunch box, putting it back in my bag and making my way to the first lesson of the afternoon where I aim to concentrate as hard as I can, even though it's History, in order to push all other thoughts from my mind.

December, 1976

The lights are spiky, fuzzy, glowing large and shrinking again. I'm sitting on the floor, my back resting against the sofa. The television's on, but I only have eyes for the Christmas tree and its lights. Red, green, yellow, pink. I can make them warm and soft; I can make them grow. I practice unfocusing and focusing my eyes to varying degrees of fuzzy and sharp. I watch the lights all evening. The tinsel is like lights too, reflecting them, and I can do the same with that, until the whole tree is a mass of furry pointy light. It's magical.

Mum's foot swings from the sofa, bobbing to the beat of the music on the television. She has one leg tucked up underneath her, the other crossed over it and dangling down. I tried that once but it wasn't very comfortable. I prefer the floor, or the sofa as long as I can snuggle with Mum. Dad is in the armchair with his pipe. He's not allowed over here when he has a pipe on, although being a couple more feet away makes no difference to the smoke or the smell. I like the smell of his pipe, but not the smoke. It drifts up to the ceiling and hangs around in a dark cloud, moving slowly. I watch that sometimes but it's not as good as the lights.

Too soon, it's time for bed. I have to be asleep straight away or Father Christmas won't come, Mum says. I might not be able to sleep! That thought freezes my breath and Mum stops, sitting me on her lap on the bottom step.

'It's okay, Tom. Do your breathing, like we said, remember?' She does it too. In, one, two, three. Out, one, two, three. 'I'm sorry, Father Christmas will definitely come, don't worry about it!' She jiggles me on her knee, trying to cheer me up.

I look at her face, equal parts guilt and joy. 'Really, Mummy?'

'Really! That's just something people say, "You have to be asleep or he won't come," but it's not true. He comes anyway, promise.'

'Promise?'

'Cross my heart,' she draws an 'X' in the air over her

chest with a finger. I'm not sure. I think I'd better try to be asleep anyway. Too tired to resist, I let her carry me up the stairs and plonk me in the bed.

'Night, night, night, night, night...'

*

Special secret silent hours in the morning. I look at the clock in the living room; it says four something. Mum is laid on the sofa in her dressing gown. I got her up too early, she says, but she's smiling so it must be okay really. My presents are already unwrapped and I'm fighting sleep too. I feel so heavy, filled up with a fizziness and a stillness at the same time. I climb onto the sofa next to mum and look at the lights. They must have been on all night. They start to move, reaching out to each other, pulling back, reaching again, until they all go out.

We're woken by Dad's laughter as he comes into the room.

'Look at you two!' he says.

Mum jumps up, dislodging me so that I roll onto the floor, laughing too, 'The turkey!' she shrieks. 'It should have been in hours ago!'

Dad takes her place on the sofa, calling through, 'Put

the kettle on!' to Mum, and then, to me, 'So, what did Father Christmas bring you, Tommy?'

For a moment all I can do is sit there on the floor grinning at him, breathing big, happy sighs. It's too much. I can't tell him. And then I turn to the tree, where all my presents are piled up underneath like offerings, and crawl across the discarded wrapping paper, crunching and slipping, to begin the inventory.

*

After dinner, we go for a walk in the crisp afternoon. I bring my new digger with me. I've hardly put it down all day. It's the best digger in the world. The pavements have a white layer of frost on them and I puff my cheeks out, blowing air out hard, pretending to be a dragon breathing fire. The grass is wearing the frost too, on its tips. Pointy white hats on thin green wizards.

Dad looks after my digger while he and Mum swing me between them, a hand each, but it's too slippery so we stop. We walk all around the lake, saying 'Happy Christmas' to the ducks and the geese waddling about on the ice to get to a thawed out part so they can go fishing.

I think about the lights on the tree, and the swirling,

whirling pattern on the hall carpet. That's going to be a great road for my digger to go along.

Chapter Eleven

Claire isn't a pupil at this school. She attends a private school over the border in Leicestershire, travelling there and back each day in her father's Jaguar. Apparently Mrs Roberts, who is her Auntie (that's not some weird nickname she has for her or anything), asked her to spare a few hours during her holiday to come to the playing field of the village school and sit on my bench. It happened that her school holidays are different from ours, so Claire would be free to become my brand new friend and take my mind off all this silly Hag nonsense I'm getting obsessed with. Mrs Roberts explained all this to me in a phone call last night.

'Sorry Tom, I shouldn't have interfered, I see that now. It seemed like a good idea. I was trying to help! It's just you were so wrapped up in the story, and I didn't help either, I know, encouraging you and giving you those clippings and everything. But I got so worried you might be getting obsessed with it all, and it's not good for you. That panic attack you had really frightened me, Tom. I just wanted to help.' Her voice drops. 'You shouldn't get too involved in the story, Tom, it doesn't lead anywhere. And Claire's lovely, isn't she? She told me you had some lovely chats! I thought she might take your mind off it all. You shouldn't get so worked up about a silly story.'

'Silly story?' The telephone receiver is clenched in my fist. I'm desperate to hang up so I don't have to hear any more.

'Oh, haha! No, but I mean you take it all so seriously, and I just thought... Well, I thought Claire might be a nice friend for you.'

It's not funny! I want to bellow at her but I keep my lips shut tight. Claire must have relished the Famous Five notion of sneaking into a school she doesn't attend each lunch time to meet a total stranger who's such a loser that this is the only way he can make any friends. It's easy enough to sneak through the gap in the fence around the school playing field and get to the bench. Many of the children come and go through that gap, using it as a short cut to the shops or home.

With forced politeness, I say 'Thank you, Mrs Roberts. Please don't ring me again,' and hang up. She's still prattling as the receiver is on its way to the cradle, but I don't care. I'd had no idea where Claire popped up from, so unexpected, but I like her and now I discover she's not really interested in me and doesn't find me funny, or any of the other things she said, but was only there because her Auntie asked her to take pity on the poor tragic loner from her school and pretend to be my friend.

School is impossible now I don't have the blessed retreat of either the library or the bench on the playing field. I escape home for lunch most days, even when Helen or Bob are there. They don't mind, although they repeatedly remind me it's too far to come for such a short time. I never do talk to Helen about it. I can't think of a way to frame that conversation in any way that would not make her think I had completely lost my marbles. So, I still have no idea how much she knows about the Hag, the body, or any of the rest of it.

At the moment, it's the shadows that intrigue me more than anything. The Hag and the body have a link to reality, no matter how fragile, but the shadows are something else. There are no newspaper clippings mentioning those, I'm sure, and whereas most children in Annisthorpe would have come across the story of the Hag in the Woods at some point, there is never any mention of the shadows.

I'm pushing my Weetabix around in the bowl when I realise that Helen has asked a question to which she's awaiting a response. I look up and half shrug, half smile at her.

'Sorry Gran, did you say something?' I try to sound less destitute than I feel.

'Tom, I think you should have a couple of days off school. Rest, get yourself together a bit. You know.'

'Oh,' I study my half-eaten breakfast. 'Well, I don't like school, as you're aware,' I can't keep the smile from broadening on my face. 'So, that would be nice.' I envision the next two days stretching out before me. I can stay in my room and have a reading marathon. I called at the village library on Monday so have plenty of books to try out.

Helen can't let it go that easily. 'Is there anything you want to talk about, Tom?'

'No,' I say too quickly, sullen again. I scrape my chair back and take the steps two at a time to get to my room and get into my jeans and t-shirt for the day. I go to the pile of books from the library, stacked on top of the chest of drawers, obscuring Bananarama on the wall. I close my eyes and let my finger fall on a random spine. The Flamingo's Smile by Stephen Jay Gould. Perfect. I take it to my bed and lie on my front, propped up on my elbows, to read.

It's a couple of hours later when the post arrives and there, on the doormat, which I ran down to see (getting a bit bored, to be honest) is a letter addressed to me. I hardly ever get letters. It is handwritten, with a local post mark.

I take it upstairs, leaving the rest of the mail on the doormat untouched, and sit on the bed. My book, open upside down to keep my place, bounces as I add my weight to the mattress. I study the envelope for a long time, shifting back to get comfortable, leaning my back against the wall by the window. I turn the envelope over a few times in my hands. I don't recognise the writing. The envelope is thin, not much in it, most likely only one sheet of paper. The paper of the envelope is too thick for me to be able to see anything of the contents without opening it, which annoys me a bit. I lean forward and put the letter on the bedside table, on top of The Return of the King, my current bedtime reading, sit back and look at nothing in particular.

There is a fizzy sensation in the pit of my belly that turns and twists. This letter can't be good. I contemplate taking it outside and putting it into the dustbin without opening it. Instead, I lean forward again to pick it up and rip it open, getting it over with quickly, like taking a plaster off. My nails, bitten to the quick, struggle with the paper and instead of a neat opening at the top of the envelope, I end up shredding it, creating three long tears across its width. Once in, I draw a breath, and retrieve the paper from inside. I was right: one sheet, folded in half.

'Dear Tom,

Hello, I hope you are well. It's Claire here, Mrs Roberts' niece. I wanted to write to you to apologise about what happened. I feel dreadful about it. I'm sorry.

I admit, I did think it would be fun to take part in Auntie Sue's secret mission for me, but I never imagined the consequences for you. There are children at my school who are shy and struggle to made friends, and even get bullied, so I should have realised it would be like that at your school too. When Auntie Sue told me about it, it sounded like such a fun thing to do on my holiday, like a little project.

I think of you as a friend now though, a real one, Tom and I'd like to go to the Old Wood and see the spot where the body was. I've been having terrible dreams since you told me about the Hag and the shadows. Anyway, as the wood is kind of your place, I wanted to ask if you'd like to come too. I don't really want to go on my own, and you would be the perfect companion for it. I really am very sorry about what happened. I hope we can still be friends. I miss our chats.

I'll be at the Old Wood on Saturday, 12 noon, so if you'd like to come too, I'll meet you by the gate.

Well, I can't think what else to say, so I'll leave it at that. Sorry again, I hope you are okay.

Claire.'

I read the letter through one more time. She must have written it ever so fast and dashed to catch the last post. This makes me think she's genuine, but I'm not sure. Despite this, I'm already certain that I'll be there, at the gate to the Old Wood, at noon on Saturday.

Chapter Twelve

The next morning there's a knock at the door. It's ten past nine and I'm still in my pyjamas, reading in bed. Helen answers and I'm sure I hear Claire's voice outside, right underneath my window. The door closes and the voice is inside, more muffled, moving through to the living room. I panic, flinging the book aside, and get to my feet. Dashing to the bathroom for an emergency pee, I hope she doesn't glance up and see me running about on the landing in my pyjamas, or hear all the commotion. In the bathroom, I splash water on my face and try to get the last bit out of the hair gel tube, squeezing till my fingers turn white, to get my hair to do something less embarrassing. I fumble and twist at my curls, but afterwards it still looks the same as before. Giving up, I brush my teeth and head back to the bedroom to get dressed.

'I'll just see if he's up!' Helen's on her way up the stairs. I sit on the bed and open my book at the wrong page, trying to look like I was here all along. She taps and puts her head round the door.

'Morning Tom,' she beams. 'You've got a visitor!'

'Uh, who is it?' I try to look innocent.

'A girl from school, she said. Claire. Very pretty.'

I roll my eyes. 'Okay, I'll be there in a minute'

Helen goes back downstairs and I sit on the bed, staring at the carpet. I get Claire's letter out and scan it for clues. She didn't say anything about coming round here today. Eventually, there's nothing else for it, I have to go down and speak to her.

After many mumbled greetings, shy laughs, and one more apology from Claire, we walk together towards the Old Wood. Claire is doing most of the talking, which is a relief as I'm more tongue-tied than usual. Her hair keeps catching in the wind and blowing into my face. I like that, and make no effort to move further away from her to prevent it happening. It smells of strawberries. She must be a fan of those fruity shampoos I've seen in the corner shop.

She talks and talks, waving her arms to emphasise

this point or that point, until I'm reminded of the way Sue talked on our walk back to the bus station that day, when I was struggling to breathe and she overcompensated by waffling a load of nonsense the whole time. The smile disappears from my face and the whipping hair irritates me for the first time. I don't want to think about Mrs Roberts. I like Claire a lot, but I can't trust her. Not yet. There is an invisible barrier between us as we walk along.

'The dreams are getting awful, Tom.'

'Really? Still about the shadows and everything?'

'Yes. Much worse though.' Her face clouds over. I steer her towards the wall that surrounds the Old Wood - we're nearly at the gates already - where we both perch. I'm ready to forgive her now, she looks so upset.

'Tell me,' I say.

'Yes, I owe you that at least. Sorry about all the confusion again, I don't understand what Auntie Sue's thinking sometimes, and I shouldn't have agreed to it. It just sounded fun.' I say nothing.

'It's ridiculous really. It's not going to sound scary or anything, but there's something about these dreams that makes me so tense and moody, even my mother's noticed. She keeps saying I must have my period, but it's not that.' I screw my nose up at this unwanted information. 'In one particular one you're there, and Sue, and we're in a huge mansion somewhere. There are shadows all around, climbing up every wall and surface, spreading out over the cold oak floor, circling around the door-knobs and reaching towards the light fittings in the ceiling.' This sounds familiar. That is exactly how the shadows act. The story of her dream draws me in, as stories always do. Claire is staring into the middle distance as she talks, as though she sees the dream there.

'It's light in the room, despite all the shadows, and I can see everything clearly. It makes me think of one of those dramas they sometimes put on the television on a Sunday evening. Miss Marple or somebody trying to solve a mystery, everybody sitting around not really doing much, too much talking.

'We are all seated, me, you and Sue, when the door-knob turns and a man I don't recognise comes in. He's large, tall and broad, and doesn't speak, but moves quickly into the room, coming straight towards us. He stops the other side of this little round side table that's there, with an ornate old lamp on it, and sways on his feet. The shadows like the man. They all swarm to him as soon as he comes in, following him to the table and when he stops they consume him, riding up his sides and onto his face and hair, smothering him in darkness.

'The man becomes a shadow, sort of a negative of himself. Then his eyeless face looks at us all, studying us each in turn for a long time, before he turns and goes back the way he came. The shadows go with him, so there is nothing more remarkable to see than an Edwardian drawing room with three startled people in it.

'He slams the door, and the glass in the chandelier over our heads tinkles. Every time, I wake up, convinced I'm hearing next door's wind chime singing in the breeze. There is no sound, though.' Her hands, which have been out in front of her holding the dream so she can see it, drop to her legs, and she looks at me.

'Wow.'

'Yeah,' she says, standing to move off again. I follow her.

The trees reach over the wall to the wood, their branches barer than when I saw them last. There is a nip in the air, and we both have our coats on, me in my blue anorak and Claire in a bright red woollen coat that fastens with big buttons down the front. The contrast against her yellow hair is striking.

The old iron gates stand before us, rusting, permanently wedged half open against some unseen obstacle on the ground. The leaves bank up against the rails and the walls on both sides, growing deeper as the weeks go by despite the winds and the kicking feet of children going past.

'So,' Claire says. I wonder if she feels it too, the pull towards the wood, the urge to go to the giant beech which is not there anymore except for a hulking stump like an elephant's foot, but I don't ask.

'Shall we?' she tries again, having got no response the first time. I clear my throat, and give her a small apologetic smile. The atmosphere of the wood is different from how I remember it. There is no feeling of portent this time. I'm not sure what Claire is expecting to see, but I have a horrible feeling she will be disappointed, and it turns out I'm right. Within the hour we are leaving again, sidling through those ornate gates with nothing to show for our visit but a bunch of leaves that Claire carries in her arms. She's going to make an arrangement or picture when she gets home. I can't help feeling like a fraud, but Claire says she's not disappointed, she wanted to see the wood, that's all, having never been in there before.

We talked more about her dreams while we were at the stump, walking around and around it, avoiding eye contact.

'It's probably hearing the stories about Hags and shadows has been playing on my mind. I don't think it means anything,' Claire said. I think we both see it must be more than that, but I don't say anything to avoid sounding foolish.

'I really hope we can still be friends,' she says as we head off back down the street. I'm tight-lipped. She laughs. 'You're a bit sullen, but there's something about you, Tom. You're like a faithful old dog, never saying anything, but always there, loyal to the last.'

'Erm. Okay.' The blush is there again, and I roll my eyes at it, powerless to do anything else. To my intense relief, Claire changes the subject and returns to her usual self, chatting away about nothing in particular.

We walk back to my house. I don't especially want

her to come back with me, having endured her nattering and this awkwardness for long enough, and that hair which she doesn't even attempt to control. But when she suggests it, I can't think of a thing to say to discourage her.

I hate myself for my inability to think quicker. It's a sport for me, hating myself. I have to aim for ever greater heights. I carry it with me all day like a security blanket and at night, in sleep, it falls away to the floor, waiting to be picked up again in the morning.

Helen is in when we get back, the creaking front gate giving away our arrival. Her small face appears at the window, accompanied by a timidly waving hand. The wind swirls and a few strands of Claire's hair stick to my bottom lip. I flick them aside, making spitting noises, and Claire gives me a quizzical look. Leaves skitter around the small, paved garden. I watch them for a minute before opening the door.

Soon, Claire and I are in my room looking at the newspaper clippings Sue gave me, and consuming the cans of Coke and sandwiches Helen brought up for us.

My shoulders drop, millimetre by millimetre, as time goes on and chatting with Claire gets easier. She likes the clippings for the same reasons that I do. Not because of any information they contain, but because of their ancient fustiness, and the way they have turned into fabric, no longer paper, over time.

We both sit on the bed, me at the head end and Claire way down at the foot end, with the clippings between us. I show her my 'Old Wood' notebook, which I have neglected to write in since the day I started it.

Claire is as intrigued by the shadows as I am, especially as they keep appearing in her dreams as one solid mass, that of a large man. Claire wonders aloud who that man might be, but I have no answer to that. We have a chuckle at how spectacularly Sue's plan has backfired. She wanted to put me off the story of the Hag, but all she's achieved is creating another young person who is as interested in it as I am.

The window is slightly open - I can't stand a stuffy room - and wisps of breeze come through, making the net curtain billow out across the bed. The sun has come out, but it's at the back of the house. It would be lovely in the back garden this afternoon, but my room remains shady and cool.

'In a funny way, I wish I could see the shadows in

real life too,' Claire says. My face must have a warning on it because she stops and puts her hand up to her neck.

'They're all right to start with, but after a while it's not so much fun, believe me.'

'Oh, I know, I didn't mean... I'm just thinking aloud. I wouldn't want it at all really, but in a funny way I wish I were having the experience in the same way that Auntie Sue and you did. She's not so bad, you know, my Auntie Sue. She just tries to help sometimes and gets it all wrong. That's what happened.' I'm willing to believe that, but to forgive it is another matter. Claire looks down at her hands, pushing her cuticles back as she's talking. 'All I get are these weird dreams, I just thought it would be good to have the same experience as others. And I get this awful feeling of dread, like something tightening around my chest, like the walls closing in.'

Hours later, after Claire has gone home for her dinner, I can't imagine what we found to talk about for so long. It wasn't all about the shadows and the stories, though they cropped up often. As Claire noticed things around my room we got to talking about those, and I put a film on at one point but it ran its course gossiping in the background with us two ignoring it as we went onto another topic, or looked at the clippings again. I try to go over everything I said to check I didn't give too much away, but I can't remember most of it. I feel vulnerable and exposed. But Claire has given me no reason not to trust her this day.

*

Months later there is an inter-school sports tournament that institutions from the whole county are expected to take part in. Like everyone else from my year at school, I'm required to be there, despite not taking part in any of the sports. I am a reluctant observer, and not the only one. Even some of the school bullies are drifting around looking displaced, suddenly aware of their place in society by virtue of the presence of so many other bullies from other schools whose modus operandi is unknown to them. I've never seen them so quiet.

I amble through the crowd of people who are standing around waiting for something to happen, glad for the day off school but wishing I didn't have to spend it here. I try not to think about all the things I'd rather be doing with my time and instead decide I might as well try to get to the front to see what's going on.

I weave around people, self-conscious in my ordinary clothes, jeans and a t-shirt, among all these schooly types whom, if they've noticed me before, will have seen me in my school uniform that still smells of the shop we bought it from despite the many washings it's had since.

The hems of my jeans scuff the grass and I try to act casual, hands in pockets. I have no idea how to behave in a context like this, and not much desire to learn. Why I couldn't have spent the day at home reading or researching something I can't say. I couldn't care less if my classmates triumph or fail, and I notice that some of those actually participating find it nearly as hard to drum up any enthusiasm for it, standing in groups, complaining.

Announcements come over a Tannoy system, made by a man who gushes so much about what events are coming up and who has won what already that his voice is distorted in his rush to get the words out. The day has barely started and it's beginning to overwhelm me already. My head swims with the crowds, noise and heat.

I get to the front of the crowd, the sun beaming like a laser onto one particular patch of my head where my sort-of parting is to super-heat it in a way that irritates me intensely. I put my hand up to that spot so my fingers can take the heat instead, and then lower it to shield my eyes, feeling ridiculous. Someone who knew what they were doing would have a hat with a visor, or a pair of sunglasses or something, but no, not me, I don't think of things like that. Instead, I have to keep putting my hand up above my eyes as if attempting some lame salute to the efforts of the participants on the field.

We are waiting for a football match to start, and there's a gaggle of girls on the pitch performing a dance routine in the style of American cheerleaders. I'm only half watching, and their leg-kicking, pom-pom shaking dance is nearly over before it dawns on me why one of the girls looks so familiar.

That yellow hair is tied back in a pony-tail. I've never seen it like that before. I didn't expect to see her here. I had almost forgotten about the meetings and unusual conversations of the previous year. And I'd forgotten that she told me she took dance classes. I watch the end of the routine with far greater interest than before, whilst trying to be cool and disinterested at the same time, which doesn't seem to be possible. I'm trying to be invisible, and just as I'm thinking I'd better make my way further back into the crowd, our eyes lock for a second. Her smile expands when she sees me, making sure I know she's spotted me, before returning to the eyes-front, fixed grin expression the dance requires.

There's a flurry of pompoms and tiny skirts as the dance winds up, all red and white stripes and legs, after which the girls mill around, unsure what they are supposed to do next. I hear snatches of their conversation, the upshot of which is that they are off duty for a little while. They disperse after their nattering and giggling dies down. They are all like Claire, chattering easily, hair everywhere.

I'm not sure why I'm standing here looking over at them when the routine finished ages ago and the group has disintegrated into their separate factions: a bunch of girls standing about who happen to be wearing the same red tops and little bouncy skirts. I realise what I'm doing too late as Claire is already walking over to me. I stand my ground, hating the flush that's creeping up from under my t-shirt to soak my neck in its lurid red. Every cell in my body rages at me to turn and go, duck my head, get out of here, she's coming, and she's going to want to talk! In a fantastic display of will over instinct, I hold her gaze as she gets closer, and produce what I hope looks like a convincing smile.

'Tom!' She's waving, and my mind flits to the Stevie Smith poem I'd mentioned to Mrs Roberts. She liked that. She thought it fit perfectly. Not Waving But Drowning. Then I see the body in the woods, early last autumn, her limp hand waving. It feels so long ago, like it happened to someone else and I only heard about it. Claire is right in front of me, the smile dropping from her lips. I realise she said something, and is being made to wait too long for my response while I'm daydreaming about dead waving hands. For the hundredth time today, I feel like an idiot.

'I'm sorry, what did you say?'

She laughs, throwing her head back. Then, as though addressing a particularly dim toddler, she repeats, 'How. Have. You. Been?'

I laugh too. 'Fine thanks,' I lie. 'You?'

'Yeah, great. I'm just here with the dancers from my school. We got hired to do this sports do, isn't that brilliant?' Her smile fades. 'Sorry about all that stuff last year.' Her hands push over to her side, sweeping away last year like so many leaves piled against a wall.

'That's okay. Funny old episode,' I say, realising I sound like Granddad again. 'It's all done with now, no need to mention it.' I wish she hadn't.

'I've got a few minutes before I have to do anything. Are you actually interested in this football match, or shall we hang out for a bit?'

'Um, yeah, okay.'

'I don't know if there's a nice little bench here or...' She's pretending to look around for one, her pony-tail swishing back and forth, and I can't help laughing. She punches me on the arm and saunters off. I fall in next to her, like we're old friends. She's the closest thing I've got to that, anyway. We're aiming for the perimeter of the field.

In a rare moment of exuberance (the weather must be getting to me) I splurt out, 'What fresh Hell is this?' in mock horror, 'some kind of huge, communal sports day?' I put as much vitriol as I can muster into the last two words, for enhanced comic effect, and Claire doesn't disappoint, letting out a peel of ringing laughter that makes her pony-tail bounce and shake. I'm a big fan of shoehorning my favourite phrases into my speech, even if my speech is so rare you might not think there'd be room for anything that isn't totally necessary. 'What fresh Hell is this?' is a new one. I heard it on a comedy programme over a week ago, and now I have to say it every opportunity I get, whether it's relevant or not. I don't think I'll ever tire of it. At least, not until my next favourite phrase comes along. I'm chuckling with Claire until we fall into an amiable silence.

A little too late, she responds, 'Yes, not really your sort of thing is it? They should have an inter-school library... scholarship...' she struggles for the right words '... thing for you,' and we both laugh.

'Yes, that would be good.' Seriously, that's a good idea.

I look in towards the field where various sporting events are happening all at once. The sun has faded as thin clouds cover the sky. There are too many smells; the rubber of plimsolls, the more sterile scent of brand new trainers for the serious pupils (or the ones with more money), the sweat pooling on t-shirts, the grass, fresh cut for the occasion, green and compliant under all these feet; and closer, emanating from Claire, the faint floral aroma of her deodorant or perfume that makes me think of Mum, rushing up and down the hall, getting ready to go out for the evening.

All that activity, all at once, and the dirt in the air coming from the shouting mouths, so urgent, 'John, to me!', 'Go on, Cheryl!', 'Pass! Pass!' They cloud the air around them with their breath and their stench. I have to look away, back to Claire, ignorant of all this going on in my head, smiling vaguely to herself. I notice she's not wittering on today like she normally does, and for that, I'm thankful.

To our delight, we find a bench, and it's right in the corner of the field. I joke that maybe there's a law we don't know about which states all school playing fields must have a pointless bench in the corner for losers to sit on. Claire laughs, but says her school doesn't have one so that's not true. We sit on the bench.

'You know, I've been thinking I'll go back to the woods soon. Take my camera again. I bet it's really pretty in the spring, I've never seen it at this time of year. I wonder if there are bulbs, and flowers."

'I'd like to see that film if you do.' Claire is kicking her feet, scuffing the grass with her pointed toes encased in brilliant white plimsolls, which don't quite reach the ground. My feet are planted solid in the grass.

'I'll show it to you.'

We both gaze into our separate middle distances.

'I never showed you the first one, I just thought. Mind you, there's not much to see.'

'I did believe you, about the body and everything,' Claire looks at me.

'I know.' I find a single point to fix on in the field, like a person out at sea staring at a point on the horizon, determined to keep the sickness away. 'It all got a bit mad and...' I trail off without bothering to finish. We both know what happened.

'I still have the dreams,' I look at her, eyebrows raised. I assumed they must have stopped ages ago. 'I've got used to them now - it's only about once a week or something - but usually the same sort of thing as before. Shadows that become a man, something to do with the Hag, but I can't work out what. You and Auntie Sue are always there,' She flicks her fringe out of her eyes with a delicate finger, 'So, it's all your fault.' She punches me on the arm again. This appears to be her new gesture. I like it. It has a conspiratorial edge, like we're sharing a joke that only us two would get.

'Sorry about that. Mrs Roberts should never have brought you into it, it was bad enough just me and her getting all obsessed.'

'I don't see her much anymore. She, um, my mother said we wouldn't see her much anymore. I'm not sure why.' I don't push it.

We sit for more moments, watching the activity on the field. I try to ride over the top of it with my eyes so as not to drown. Claire has to get back, she's due on dance duty in a few minutes.

'You should make that film, Tom, and I'd really like to see it when you do. Make sure you tell me when it's done!' She's getting up, drifting away. I remain seated. Now that I've found a bench I think I'll stay here until it's time to go. It's nice in this corner and if I remember to keep the top joint of the goal posts as my anchor point, the arms and legs and shouts and life of the sports field won't overwhelm me.

'You could come with me!' I had no idea I was going

to say it until it was out of my mouth, but I don't regret it.

Claire, who had turned and was walking away, whips back around, that yellow pony-tail flying behind her. She's beaming.

'Do you know, I think I'd like that.' She cocks her head as though the idea hadn't occurred to her before, and she likes it. 'I will. When are you going?'

I have no idea. 'Er, this Saturday?'

'Great, about twelve again? I'll see you there, at the gates.' She gives one last, extra big smile before turning and keeping walking away from me this time, pony-tail swishing from side to side, tiny skirt bouncing.

Chapter Thirteen

Events conspire to ensure Claire and I do not see each other that weekend, nor any weekend in the near future. First Helen is taken ill, and I want to stay at home to help look after her, then Claire has some function to attend for the dance class she does - another grade in ballet, I think. I gave her my phone number so we can ring each other to hear what our excuses are this time. This goes on for weeks, until it becomes impossible to continue without both of us admitting we're regretting the rashness of our talk on that sports day and have been trying to get out of it. We have to either admit this or, finally, meet.

It's the summer holidays by the time we run out of excuses, infeasible illnesses and pressing commitments we can't possibly get out of, and agree to meet. The sun has been riding high for days, baking the earth and browning or burning the inhabitants' skin.

I spend most of the time in my room, which is on the north side of the house, so enjoys a cooler temperature in the long afternoons. I like to have the windows wide open and let the net curtains billow into the room.

Occasionally I go and sit in the garden instead, taking my book or some homework, and sit on the bench by the back hedge, alternately reading a line or two and glancing up at a bird flying overhead to get to the feeders by the shed, or at Bob, who painstakingly tends to his vegetables, lumbering back and forth between the veg patch and the shed with various implements, bits of string, plant pots, or nothing.

Sometimes he forgets what he went for, and gets all the way back to the veg patch before he remembers, and has to turn back for another try. This is happening more often lately. He forgets things that everyone knows, like who the Prime Minister is, or what date Valentine's Day is, and sometimes I go into a room to find him standing in the middle of the carpet with a lost expression and no idea why he's there. Helen looks after him, concealing the worst symptoms the best she can.

I arrange to meet Claire in the centre of the village, by the old war memorial. The day is humid, with no movement in the air. The sun beams down relentlessly, as it has done for weeks with only a couple of grey days that threaten rain to break the monotony.

Claire arrives on time. I'm leaning against a garden wall, getting half-eaten by overgrown ivy. My camera is in its bag over my shoulder, and I'm in jeans and t-shirt, the same as Claire, who steps lightly across the road, calling a sing-song 'Hellooo,' to somebody she knows on the other pavement. The man turns after Claire has passed him to let his eyes linger a second too long on her legs as she sashays across the road to meet me. Her hair is loose. I don't know how she can she stand it all around her face in this heat.

Claire looks different from the last time we met, and I wonder if I do too. We've both grown a tiny bit, both turned fifteen and both become leaner, somehow. As we fall into step beside each other, ambling towards the woods, I see that there is a darkness under her eyes that wasn't there before.

Claire is talking about her school and all the things she's been up to in the last term or so, filling the silence with people I don't know and details I don't care about, making over the top gestures to emphasise every point she makes. After a few minutes, she stops.

'Sorry, you're not interested in all that. I went into overdrive then!' A small giggle. 'So, how have you been, then?'

'I'm okay. Just the same really,' I'm always regretting that I can't be more interesting for people. I never have anything to tell them. 'Are you still having those dreams?'

Her face darkens. 'Yes, nearly every night. They're getting worse, and sometimes I don't want to go to sleep because of them. I stay up really late to avoid going to sleep and having another one.'

'I'm sorry about that. If I'd never gone blabbing to your Auntie about it all, and she hadn't got you involved, you would probably still be sleeping soundly every night, blissfully unaware.'

'It's not your fault, but we don't see Auntie Sue anymore. I think Mum's cross with her, although I'm not sure why. It might be this; the woods and everything. They've been separated for a while, my mum and dad. They've just decided to try again, for me, they said.' She pulls a face to suggest she's not sure that's a good idea. 'They're not telling me anything, no matter how much I ask, so I don't know if the problems they're having are anything to do with Auntie Sue, as it's all being left to my imagination. I haven't seen or heard from her for months. I do wonder how she is.' She appears to be asking the sky, tilting her head back and closing her eyes. The heat is pounding down on us, and haze comes off the road like steam off a hot bath. 'I suppose I could ring her and ask.' She looks ahead again, swinging her arms as she strolls along next to me.

'They've told me not to contact her, but I don't know why and I don't see how they can stop me. They might not even find out, unless she told them. Have you seen her at school?'

'Only from a distance. I don't like going to the library there anymore. It doesn't feel right, although I'm not really angry with her now. It would be awkward, though. There's a nice library in the village so I go there instead. They're used to me.'

'Do you think I should ring her?'

'I don't know. I keep feeling like I should talk to her

too. But what would I say?'

'I don't like her being cut off. I mean, what did she really do that was so wrong? She tried to help, and as often happens when Auntie Sue tries to help, it all went wrong. But she's not a bad person, and it's really unfair of Mum and Dad to treat her like this. I keep thinking maybe I should check she's okay, regardless of what they say.'

'I don't see why you shouldn't. It might put your mind at rest, and you might be able to sleep better afterwards.'

Claire glances across at me, a half smile on her lips, 'You're very perceptive, for a boy.' I have no clue what to say to that, so I try to imitate her half smile back at her.

'Okay, next time Mum and Dad go out and leave me for a bit - they do that quite a lot, I love it - I'll give Auntie Sue a ring and make sure she's okay. She's a bit of a wally sometimes, but I do like her, and I miss her. Always had a soft spot for my Auntie Sue, I did.'

Even the cars are lazy in the heat, thrumming along as if it's all too much effort for them. We cross to the wall surrounding the wood. Around the next bend we will find those familiar rusty gates, eternally half-open, as though unsure whether to close up for business or not.

As we're approaching the corner, Claire stops walking for no reason that I can see, her eyes fixed on part of the wall. I look from Claire to the space she is looking at, the junction between the wall and the pavement where the tarmac meets the red crumble of bricks, about six feet ahead of us. There are two chocolate wrappers there, dropped by people too idle to find the nearest waste bin. There is one not twenty five yards from this spot. Claire is moving back until she stops, eyes fixed on that same spot.

'Can you see that?' Her voice is a note higher than usual.

I turn back to the part of the wall she's looking at, following her eye-line the best I can, and move towards it, in case her eyes are better than mine and she's seeing something tiny that's eluding me. I crouch down by the wall to get a better look, reaching out to the bricks.

'See what?' I have to ask finally, unable to fathom what she means.

'The shadow.'

I spring back to my feet, panic birthing in my belly. 'No,' my voice is heavy, 'I can't see anything.' I go back to Claire, wanting to put my arm around her, but it remains fixed to my side in an awkward paralysis. I clear my throat and attempt to keep my breathing normal.

'Claire, there's nothing there.' But I know there is.

'There is. There's one of the shadows I've been seeing in my dreams.'

We're attracting the attention of passers-by, standing in the middle of the pavement looking at the wall. I manage to move my arm enough to tap her on the elbow.

'Come on, let's keep moving.' I try my best to sound calm, but if there are shadows here, and I have no reason to disbelieve her, that means they are back, at least for Claire, for the first time since that day I found the body in the woods. I haven't seen nor dreamt of them since. They've finished with me, but may be only starting with Claire. We move together in tiny, stilted steps. Claire edges around the spot where she can see the shadow, which she says is still there, as though she's expecting it to jump out at her from the wall.

It's one shadow, I tell myself, it doesn't mean anything. But I'm unable to crush the rising panic in my chest, thinking about what happened the last two times children could see these shadows and were drawn into the woods. As we round the bend, approaching the gates to the wood, Claire slows again.

'There are more of them,' she whispers.

'I can't see them, Claire,' I want to believe the fact that I can't see them means they are not really there and that Claire is imagining things, but I know better than that. I try to face up to it and not shy away. The shadows are here, and we're going to the wood whether we like it or not. They will pull us in, and all I can do is try to think of ways to deal with what's bound to happen next.

'You know what happens,' I begin, but Claire is ahead of me.

'Yes, they lead you to a body in the wood that isn't really there.' She pauses, glancing behind, and catches her breath, 'At least I know what to expect.' She sounds panicky, and I'm struggling with my own breathing, but determined to get it under control.

'There are more behind us, aren't there?' I gasp, in

between breaths.

'Yes. There are lots. They're doing that morphing and changing thing. I'm so sick of seeing them doing that, but at least usually I'm asleep and will wake up at some point.' She gives a nervous laugh before, with effort, settling her face into a brave smile, 'No going back now.'

'No,' I lean against the wall. I have to take a minute to get my breathing under control and, no longer caring how stupid I look in front of Claire, I labour over my breathing exercises, concentrating on only that for the next moment or two. Claire comes over and puts her hand on my forearm where it leans against the wall. She doesn't say anything, but waits for me to be ready and for my breathing to calm down, her face serious and concerned, before moving off, leading the way to the gate.

I follow, unsteady but determined not to show myself up too much. I'm so tired of that - of being the butt of everyone's jokes, of being looked at in that pitying or mocking way by people who could not care less about me, except as some type of amusement for them. I doubt Claire thinks of me like that, although she could have done the first few times she met me, that week last year at school. My breathing returns to normal, and my vision clears. I see no shadows, but it's clear from her demeanour that Claire does.

We pause at the gate, like the last time we were here together. It's the kind of gate that people pause at, with the way it is permanently half open, towering over you as if looking down at you asking, 'Are you sure?' I think it only grudgingly allows entrance to the woods beyond, as though it is being made to by some nagging relative but doesn't agree with this action one bit. They can't have moved in years, those gates, and I'm not sure if they can anymore.

But there's no need to bother trying to open them wider, or close them shut. The developers are on their way with their flimsy little houses, and that will be the end of the gates for good, and much more besides. I save a tiny piece of my heart to harbour the hope that they will get here and change their minds, or decide to at least leave the old wall and these gates and a few of the trees - maybe only build half the houses they were planning to.

The gates are at once imposing, eerily still, and

fragile. They are alive with the history of the woods. Claire is ahead of me, already past the gates and in the woods, and I rush to catch up.

'Are they still here?'

'Yes, there are more of them all the time. They're swarming. They're doing what we expected them to,' she whispers, maybe worrying that the shadows are listening, although I don't think they can hear us.

Nothing moves: not a branch or leaf, nor a blade of grass. The air is denser under the trees, losing heat but gaining a clamouring humidity. The sunlight out on the street cuts through that atmosphere and makes it feel lighter, but in here, with the sun struggling to get through the thick canopy overhead, the air hangs immobile, festering where it is.

The wood looks different from how I remember it. In my mind, it is always late summer here, having that used-up air of the turning of the seasons, like the aftermath of a party before anyone has tidied up and cleared away. I love the slide into autumn after summer, but today it's mid-summer and the air is different. The leaves cling onto their freshness, the cow parsley and nettles burgeoning, not yet drooping.

There is more litter this time, I can't help noticing. Other people have been here. To most people this place is a waste ground, somewhere to go to escape the gaze of all the houses and cars. It's only to people like me and Mrs Roberts, and Claire too I suppose, and Helen, that it is this living entity that's come alive in our minds.

We amble through the woods, weaving through the ashes and the limes, around a sprawling yew with its spiky needles thrusting out at us, offering us poisonous berries.

'The shadows are all around us now,' I have to stay close to Claire so that I can hear her. 'They're black and constantly changing. They get taller than us and then shrink down to the height of the rodents that must scuttle about in the undergrowth here at night. They're shape shifting into other animals, and abstract lines that I don't recognise.' She looks around herself, eyes wide. 'At a guess, there are about thirty of them. It's hard to tell, they keep overlapping and separating.'

My shoulders hunch with the frustration of not being able to see them myself, as I imagine what Claire's describing, the shadows encircling us as we make our way through the wood, ever changing. It sounds the same as when I could see them last year. I have to trust her as she is the one with the power here. I can't see what she can. I have to trust that or else I'm here in the woods with a girl I don't know all that well who is pretending to see things, and I don't want to think about that. Claire stops and I stumble into the back of her, catching her heel under my foot.

'Sorry,' I mumble, but she's looking all around herself and doesn't hear me. Her gaze sweeps over my head. I start to turn around before remembering that would be pointless.

I notice the darkness under her eyes is more pronounced since entering the wood. She looks older, more serious, but it's darker in here anyway; maybe I do too.

Claire is silent, giving me time to ponder the shadows, allowing my imagination to produce monsters that are likely far worse than what is actually here. I ponder whether the people who see the shadows are seeing a separate set each time, which exist only for them, if they are more like some kind of immortal entity which reappears periodically to specific people for reasons it keeps to itself.

Claire's feet don't move, but her upper body twists and turns to follow the shadows. Her breathing becomes shallower, her shoulders rising and falling with thin breaths, and I recognise the first signs of a possible panic attack. I'm used enough to those. I take hold of her hand with no thought for the appropriateness of that action. It's the easiest part of her to get hold of.

'Claire, remember, we've both seen the shadows, and Mrs Roberts has too. This has happened before, and I think it's happening the same way as it did those times. So, we know what to expect, yes?' I'm trying to get her to look at me, to focus on my eyes rather than whatever it is she's seeing over my shoulder and all around us from the ground right up to the tree tops. 'Claire,' I tug lightly at her hand. Her gaze flits to my face and then away again. 'Claire!' She blinks, holding her eyelids closed for a couple of beats, and turns her head to me, inch by inch.

'I have to count. I have to keep watching.' Her voice is far, far away, and her eyes drift over to my left as she's talking.

'No you don't, Claire,' I tug at her hand, harder this time. Another blink and she looks me full in the face. I speak quickly, unsure how long I'll have her attention for.

'It's not real. The shadows are not real. Right now, you are the only one who can see them. They're going to lead you, and me because I'm not leaving you alone in here, to the giant beech stump, remember? They're going to do what they always do. They'll take you to the stump. You'll probably see a body under lots of leaves. It's not really there, and nor are the leaves. It's all an illusion, Claire. Try to stay calm. None of it is real.'

She's shaking her head. 'But...'

I let go of her hand and turn towards the place where the giant beech stump is, and where the ridge lies beyond, with its hidden bower. There is panic on Claire's face, 'Tom, the shadows!'

'What?' If I could see the shadows I'd be able to cope better, but having to guess where they are guided only by what Claire's doing and what she says when she remembers to, is driving me crazy. She has not moved for minutes on end, except for her head turning this way and that, making her hair flick idly in the heavy air. But now she's only looking at me as I keep moving, walking backwards towards the stump, away from her.

'They're all around you Tom, they want you to go to the stump!'

'Good!' My arms are out, palms out towards Claire, shoulders edging up to my ears, 'Good! Let's go then! Let's go to the stump and see that body, then the shadows can all bugger off like they always do, and we can go home.'

Claire's eyes move to the camera bag slung over my shoulder. I had forgotten all about it, and I think she had too, until now. She's calmed a fraction - maybe my words have had time to sink in - but her gaze can't rest for long on any one thing.

'Take your camera out, Tom, you should film this. Maybe... maybe, if before the camera didn't pick up what you could see, then maybe this time, if you can't see the shadows, maybe...'

My hands are already gripping the bag and lifting it up in front of me before her words trail off, and my eyes widen as I catch her meaning, gaping open-mouthed at her. I can't believe I didn't think of that.

My sweaty fingers fumble with the zip. I let the bag

swing from my shoulder, wiping my hands on my jeans, and try again. I get the camera out, switch it on and hitch it up to my right shoulder, where it should have been all along. The bag falls away, light and empty, dangling from the strap trapped under the weight of the camera. I pan around, sweeping past Claire watching me, looking calmer, and try to take in as much as possible of the immediate area. Through the viewfinder, I can still see no shadows.

'No,' I say, but Claire is not discouraged, and neither am I.

'Keep filming anyway, we can check the tape later when we're less... you know.' She moves at last, her breathing normal and with more colour in her cheeks. I'm thankful to be relatively calm myself. No return of the panicky breath yet.

'I'm just going to follow the shadows,' Claire says, as if she has a choice, and glides past me as I film her. 'You come too.' Like I'm going stand here and film her walking off.

'Tell me what they're doing all the time,' I remind her.

'Yep.'

I peer through the viewfinder every so often to check I'm not accidentally filming the canopy above or the ground below, but for the most part leave the camera on my shoulder and look where I'm going, or watch Claire. She reminds me of a sleepwalker I saw in a film once, the way she's so calm, following the shadows as though she has no will of her own.

From this point, as best she can, Claire keeps up a running commentary of where the shadows are and what they are doing. Occasionally she falls silent, having apparently forgotten her task, and I have to prompt her.

Straight through the centre of the wood we go, only meandering when necessary to navigate the trees and undergrowth. Our shoes scuff through the stubbly grass, sometimes catching a discarded beer can or crisp packet, creating unnatural crunching sounds. New carrier bags decorate some of the branches, caught by their handles and destined to spend the next few months blowing inside out and back again in the winds that will eventually be back, after this heatwave has finished with us.

Claire speaks quietly and I struggle to hear. The air

is dense with the heavy greenness of the foliage all around us.

'They're mostly ahead of me. There are some still at my feet, but most of them are stretching out ahead. The line of them is becoming thinner. I think they're impatient with us. We're taking too long.'

I remember sensing what the shadows were thinking or expecting. Mrs Roberts told me she had experienced that too. I decide to call her sometime to see if she's okay. In a funny way, I'm missing her too.

'I only have one at my feet now. I think it's only one; it's hard to tell. They keep changing. I can't see the furthest ahead, it's gone too far around the trees, and there's a line of them, changing all the time, trailing back to me.'

I imagine the line of shadows stretching out in front of Claire, looking the same as they had last year when I could see them. I don't understand why they gathered around me like that earlier but I'm being ignored now. They only have one thing they want to do: get Claire to the stump. It's not me they want this time, or else I'd be able to see them - this is Claire's adventure.

I train the camera, which had veered off to the right,

capturing nothing but the density of trees and a faint impression of the red brick wall beyond which lay the main road and civilisation, back to follow Claire's progress, and perform a perfunctory check through the view finder. Nothing unusual there.

I ponder Mrs Roberts. She is involved in this in some important way that I don't understand and I feel bad for her, ostracised by Claire's family. Maybe I'll pop into the library once we are back at school and say hello to her at least. My head drops as I'm thinking so that all I see are my feet and the tops of my legs alternating step by step over the dry cracked earth. I remember where I am and jerk my head up, adjusting the position of the camera. All is as it was before, except Claire is further ahead of me than she was. I catch up with her. 'I'm going to say hello to Mrs Roberts when school's back,' I blurt out.

'Yes.' Her voice is dreamy. I don't think she's thinking about Mrs Roberts.

'I feel bad for her.'

'Yes. They're all ahead of me, I don't have any around my feet. I could reach out and touch the nearest one, but there are none touching me. Maybe I'm free?

Maybe we could turn around and leave?' She doesn't believe that any more than I do.

'No, I don't think it works like that.' I have a sudden thought, 'Claire, in your dreams, what is it that happens with the shadows again?' She's told me time and time again, but I'm so wrapped up in my own experience, the information refuses to stay in my head.

Claire stops walking and turns to face me. 'They, they... they sort of form...' She shakes her head, 'I don't want to talk about that.'

'Okay.' Sort of form... It's coming back to me, sluggish, wading through mud, but I can't get hold of it. I shrug the camera back up my shoulder and check the viewfinder. I follow Claire, as meek and helpless as a lamb following its mother.

Chapter Fourteen

I concentrate on peering through the camera's viewfinder at the back of Claire's head as she weaves through the trees, feet shushing through the grass. I'm seasick again, but keeping a close check on my breathing. Claire has forgotten she's meant to be telling me what the shadows are up to, but I don't want to remind her. I can imagine well enough what they are doing. All I want is to get to the stump, see whatever is there (or not, perhaps only Claire will see that too this time) and get out of here.

The sun strobes through gaps in the branches and leaves as I move along, stabbing daggers of light into my eyes, making me squint and look away even as I'm trying to film Claire. It does nothing to improve my mood or the sickness. I blink hard to get my eyes to focus properly, and then keep them half closed in an attempt to block out some of the dizzying effect of the sun, squinting ahead. The scene through the viewfinder is hazy as my eyes tear up in protest. I watch Claire's yellow hair jolt from side to side with each step she takes.

Claire has been silent for a number of minutes when the stump of the giant beech comes into view. I imagine the shadows streaming towards it the same way they did last year, flocking around it, swarming up the bark, magnetised to it.

I brace myself for the sight of one finger extended on the other side of the stump, beckoning to me, pale and rigid, but see nothing. Through the viewfinder, Claire is rushing. I take my eyes off her only for a second, searching for the finger, and when I look back she is not where I expect her to be, but several paces forwards, dashing for the stump. I catch up, jiggling the camera on my shoulder, and keep pace a foot or so behind her.

She reaches the stump and looks down at the patch of ground the other side that is blocked from my view, her eyes wide, her skin pale and stretched, her mouth opening to speak. The body must be there.

I catch up fast, but can't see it. It is as I thought. This time the body is for Claire. Aware of my breathing, I check the camera and point it to where Claire is looking, filming things I can't see. Nothing shows through the viewfinder but the stump, some scrubby grass, and Claire's feet moving. She's walking around the body in the same way I did last year. I can tell which parts of the body Claire is studying as she rises and falls to crouch, and then stands to take it all in.

'It's not real,' I say, but she gives no sign that she heard me. She is wrapped up in her study of the body, her hair covering her face as she bends to take in every detail. Here is the nose, here the hand, propped up against the stump. Claire waves back as if in a trance, a grotesque parody of the dead girl, before stopping and looking at her own hand as it drops to her side. Her movements are soft and slow, her face composed. Here is the scarf like a snake vanishing into the heaped up leaves, which I also cannot see, here is the toe of her boot breaking the surface.

'It's not real,' I say again.

'Can you see it?' I can barely hear her.

'No, but I know what it looks like. Claire, are the

shadows still here?' They had all vanished the moment they delivered me to the stump last autumn.

'Yes.' I take step back. 'There's something...' Claire looks over to her right, towards a thicket of ancient hawthorns all vying to cover as much land as they can with their twisting trunks. She rises from her crouched position next to the body, not taking her eyes from whatever she can see over by the hawthorns. It must be the shadows.

'They...' Her gaze shifts, moving all around her, her face a mixture of wonder and horror. It's making me panic, and my lungs quicken.

'What?' I demand.

'They, they... oohhhhhh...'

'Claire! What? What's happening?' A shallow sigh escapes and I crouch down, steadying myself against the ground with my free hand. I take two huge breaths to try and control my breathing. With my head down, all I can see is the stubbly grass and part of a root of the giant beech beyond my knees, its wrinkled skin making me think of the Hag. I can't focus on anything else until I've controlled my breathing.

Claire's trying to speak but all I hear are sounds like

somebody infinitely lost, wanting to call out but forgetting how. Her voice is coming from the other side of the stump, and I look up for long enough to see her head twisting this way and that. Her mouth is moving but I can't make out what she's saying.

I take another gulp of air and stand up, steadying my weight against the stump so I don't fall straight back down. I try to keep looking at Claire and in the directions she's looking in too, but when I do all I see are the branches and leaves and that damned sun trying to blind me. My head fizzes.

I take one more big breath, gripping onto the bark of the stump. I stride around it to where Claire is and try to catch her right wrist as it waves past me. Her head is tilted back towards something high up in the trees. Her arms float at her sides, levitating and sinking like she's treading water.

'Claire! What's happening?'

'They're... they, I mean, he, he's here...' Claire's eyes fix on one spot in the air two feet above my head. I duck and move to her side, trying to get out of the way of whatever it is that I can't see.

'Who's here? What's happening?' I catch her wrist,

trying to be gentle, and she does not resist. I don't think she notices. Her eyes move, staying at the same height, roughly two feet taller than me, but roaming across the trees and ancient hedgerows, something moving around us. Her free arm keeps on sculling. Maybe she will drown if she stops.

'He...'

I can't comprehend what happens then. It looks like Claire faints, but it's more than that. She doesn't fall, she is pushed. She is standing as she has been for a few minutes, looking up, eyes following something over her head. I have her wrist caught lightly in my left hand. The camera rests on my shoulder but I haven't checked the viewfinder in a long time. The bag swings about on my shoulder, bumping into my hip when I move. Claire is standing, and something knocks her; there can be no other reason for her falling. Something knocks her and her body caves before collapsing to the ground.

It's then that I remember. They form a man! He's here, she said! I don't let go of her wrist, so I go over too, landing on the dry earth, scraping my shin on a root of the stump. I'm able to control the fall, coming down right next to Claire and at the same time trying to stay above her and act as a shield. He has her pinned to the ground, choking for breath. I am powerless. I can't see whatever it is that's doing this, smothering her, crushing her, pushing the breath out of her.

Claire is helpless, held to the ground by something invisible. I free my hand from her wrist so I can twist around and get my body in between hers and whatever it is that's on top of her. The camera slips out of my fingers and rolls away.

Claire's struggling for breath, making dreadful choking and spitting sounds, and I'm in the impossible situation of trying to get a thing I can't see off her without crushing her further with my own body. I'm pushing against nothing but air. There is not even a ghost or a shadow to get a fix on, just thick, haze-filled air behind which the sun hammers down into my eyes.

I can't guess how long we we're there for, Claire fighting to draw air into her lungs, and me jabbing, punching and kicking at the air above her, hoping it makes a difference. It was over in seconds and went on for hours, all at once. From my position half-crouched beside Claire, I push and stab with my elbows against the air. It feels idiotic, but I must try. I can't stand by and let whatever it is suffocate her, for I'm sure that is what it's trying to do. I push and push, jab with my elbows, kick at it, try to injure it in some way, literally fighting a shadow, until at length I realise I'm no longer hearing those garbled rasping sounds coming from Claire. She has fallen silent.

I turn away from the giant invisible thing and back to Claire. She is still. As I look, my hand moving to her face, planning to check if she's breathing, there is a tickling sensation at the back of my neck. A prickly itch. Goosebumps spring up on my outstretched arm.

Something is looking at me. I think perhaps it's the shadows finally revealing themselves and snap my head around to see. In that motion, at the point where my wide open eyes pass beyond the giant stump for a fraction of a second, I see it. There, beyond the ridge the other side of the stump, low down in my sight but unmistakeable, a pair of pale rheumy eyes are looking straight at me. Without thinking, I raise myself to get a better look, conscious that I mustn't leave Claire. I half-stand, trying to protect Claire but at the same time see what this is.

I narrow my eyes against the sun and see the top half

of a face, unfathomably old and deeply creased with lines. Iron grey hair falls lifeless down the sides of her face. Those pale grey eyes do not leave mine.

I blink, the momentum keeping my head moving so I must take in as much of her as I can in a split second as my gaze passes to face where the shadow man may still be. There is nothing there that I can see, and my head returns the way it came so I can get another look at her, that dark presence beyond the ridge, but she has gone.

I don't have time to process any of this because the most pressing matter is that Claire is lying motionless on the ground beside me. For a long drawn out moment I kneel beside the inert body of my friend, my mind empty except for one repeated word, clanging like a bell. Hag.

Chapter Fifteen

Claire and I are walking back through the woods. She leans on my arm, unsteady on her feet but otherwise okay. I advise her not to talk too much, worried about the way her breathing is coming in ragged gasps.

At some point, either while standing and gazing up at a huge shadow man, or after she fell or was pushed, she fainted. She came round soon after I saw... what I saw, and tried to get up. I made her lie still for a while to make sure she wasn't hurt. Once we were both on our feet, I steadied her by her elbow in the same way that Mrs Roberts had with me that time after we met in the café. I daren't try to support her any more than that - it's too intimate - but she's soon leaning on my arm, clutching at it with sweaty fingers.

We're out from under the canopy, and losing that barrier to the sun is like an extra punishment, although

I'm pleased the strobing through the leaves has stopped. I do my best to give reassuring 'nothing to worry about' smiles to the couple of passers-by we see bestowing concerned glances in our direction. Claire's breaths are coming more naturally now, and she loosens her grip on my arm.

'Left here.' Claire's voice is faint. I steer her in that direction. 'He was just like in my dreams, Tom.' I'm concentrating hard on my own breathing, and getting Claire home. I keep my eyes fixed on the path before us, and listen hard.

'All the shadows, there were masses of them, they did the swarming thing I told you about. But at the stump, they went crazy. I couldn't... sorry, I couldn't keep talking about them.' I swallow, feeling bad for expecting her to. 'They all became one and formed this man. The man in my dreams. He was bigger than us, towering over our heads. I don't think he saw you. He was right in front of me, so tall, bending towards me. He blocked out the sun.'

'You don't have to. You shouldn't talk, Claire, it's okay. Tell me another time.'

'No, no, I have to. I'm okay now.' We stop and she

makes me turn to face her, pulling my other arm around. She drags me over to a nearby bench. We both sit. Two friends on a bench, chatting, nothing unusual here.

'He, he...'

'You don't have to.' She ignores me.

'I thought I was someone else. It's so strange. When the shadows formed that man and he loomed over me, I saw with different eyes. My skin changed. I... I don't know.' She shakes her head, 'But he was like a wave crashing over me. I couldn't do anything. All I could see were branches spinning past, leaves shrinking. My knees weakened and I felt I was falling into bed, a comfortable place. It felt like a blessing. A grave.' She frowns. 'That makes no sense.'

I say nothing.

'Coming round, the first thing I saw after you was the stump, and it looked different. It remembers, I think. It remembers the girl we saw. It knows what happened.' She's shaking her head again, her hands going up to her face. I stop her, catching her wrist ever so gently.

'It's okay, Claire. You've had a knock on the head.

We're going to get you home, okay?'

She turns on me, 'I didn't knock my head!'

'Well, you've had a shock, you can't deny that!' I'm trying to sound light-hearted.

'Hmmm,' is all she says.

I remember her address from the top of the letter she sent, which lives in the drawer with my 'Old Wood' exercise book, but I'm not sure how to get there, so she gives curt directions, saying nothing except 'Left', 'Right' and 'Cross here' all the way there.

The minute Claire opens the front door her parents are in their wide hallway, taking over from my lame attempts at caring for her. The carpet is a plush grey-blue, like a Persian cat.

There is an awkward half-conversation, where I look around at the expensive vases and antique furniture of their home and explain that we were out walking and Claire fainted, so I helped her back. Her mother's eyes narrow as I relate my tale, but she is too polite to say anything, and is more concerned with seeing her daughter is all right than with anything I say.

Both Claire's parents are surprisingly courteous, considering that here is a boy they've never met before bringing their daughter home in a worse for wear state, and complaining of a headache. Claire keeps saying there is nothing wrong and they should stop fussing, but can't hide the relief on her face when her mum suggests a sweet cup of tea and a lie down might be a good idea.

'Good thing you were there, Tom,' is the gist of Claire's father's thoughts, oft repeated in various forms on the short drive to my house. He insists on giving me a lift in his Jaguar, even though their house can't be more than fifteen minutes walk away from mine.

It's not clear if Claire told him where she was going today, or who with, but it must have been disconcerting for them to see her, pale and shocked, arrive on the doorstep with me. Her father is careful to give no outward sign of being perturbed, but I sense an undercurrent of dissatisfaction in him.

'Sounds like you two had an eventful afternoon!' It's too cheerful. He's overcompensating, his innate politeness winning out over the anger he must be feeling.

'Yes,' is all I can say, looking at the side of his face, puzzling. Claire has his profile.

He is quiet again and his mouth sets into a line, so I

shift my attention to the window at my side, watching the houses and trees whizz by. It's not until then that I feel the emptiness in my arms and realise something's missing. My camera must be in the woods where I dropped it.

I look at Claire's dad and almost burst out, 'My camera! I forgot my camera!' Luckily my mouth opens but nothing comes out. I close it, looking out of the side window, controlling myself with an effort. It's out there lying on the earth under those trees somewhere near the stump, abandoned.

For the rest of the journey, thoughts of the camera and what to do about it fill my mind. I almost forget whose car this is, and what I'm doing in it. The leather upholstery's scent is suddenly twice as strong and I long to open the window. I'm not sure which button to press, or if I'm allowed, and I don't ask.

My eyes tick right to left, right to left, as buildings and people stream past. I grab onto the handle on the door, beige and smooth. It's good to have something to hold onto in the absence of the camera bag. I draw in a large breath, trying to be subtle so Claire's dad won't see. One, two, three. I breathe out.

I clutch onto that handle all the way home, and when we get there I am deposited into our much narrower hallway by Claire's dad, who waves as he drives off with a fixed smile on his face, looking like a ventriloquist's dummy.

I force a smile myself and a quick 'Hello', but ignore the questions in Helen's eyes as I head for the kitchen to inspect the contents of the fridge. I'm starving. I assemble a sandwich and take it to the table, where Helen is seated, waiting. I'm not going to get away with not telling her what's happened, or at least a version of it.

I fill my mouth with bread to put off having to speak a little longer. Glancing out of the kitchen window, I can't believe Bob is still where I left him this morning, finding endless jobs to do in the garden, carrying on as though nothing's happened. I envy him such a simple life. All he needs are the Sunday papers, which he makes last all week, his garden, and regular cups of tea and he's a happy man. My mouth is empty again and I can't delay turning to face Helen any longer.

I astonish myself by telling her everything. The shadows, Claire's dreams, the truth of my experience in the woods last year, what happened with Mrs Roberts, the attack on Claire in the woods today, how I got her home, and the pair of eyes I saw, studying me from beyond the ridge. I'm sure they were there the whole time.

My half-eaten sandwich lays forgotten on its plate as I unload everything onto the table for Helen's inspection. She is patient and listens well, as always. She picks over the pieces and passes no judgement, remaining silent after I finish speaking. My appetite has vanished. I look up from the table to see Helen regarding me with faraway eyes.

She sighs.

Chapter Sixteen

The first thing I think of when I wake the next morning is yesterday's conversation with Helen. I've thought of little else all night, waking frequently to turn over in my bed, my head full of her voice and the jumbling thoughts of what to do about my missing camera.

She has seen it too. I should have guessed it. I knew there was something she wasn't telling me. A string of children have been enticed into the woods by the shadows over the years, Helen says, and shown the body, but nobody ever talks of it.

'I didn't see any eyes watching me, Tom, but I didn't look behind me at all, I don't think.' Her voice is quiet and frail. This is the first time she's said these words. 'I just looked at that poor girl, lying there. I didn't know what to do, so I did nothing. I ran home, all the way, we were living over by the church then, and never told a soul. I was too scared to. I think I knew it wasn't real, not really. I mean, it was real, I saw it, but I knew there wasn't really a body there under the tree and if I called the police I'd be accused of wasting their time, because they wouldn't be able to see it. And I went back another day and there was nothing there.' Her mouth quivers shut, but quickly becomes a brave little smile.

Her experience is similar to mine and Mrs Roberts', except she says she had lots of dreams about the shadows, and sometimes still does, like Claire does. I must contact Mrs Roberts soon to see if she is okay. I'll check with Claire first to see if it's all right to tell her what happened yesterday.

'If I'm honest, I guessed at most of what you've told me, Tom,' Gran said. 'Having seen the same things myself, even if it was years ago now, back when I was your age. I knew something was up, I just didn't want to believe it could be this.' She's relaxing as she talks. 'It's real now. Out in the open. No more hiding, I suppose,' she lifts her eyes, peering at me across the table. 'I've had my head in the sand for so long, it's quite a relief to finally talk about it. When it happened, I tried to forget about it, telling myself I'd passed out, or had fallen and was dreaming. I locked it away in a box in my mind and threw away the key. But now you, and this Claire especially...' she trails off and I wait, but she says no more about it after that.

The camera is out there, unless it's been taken by somebody in the night. There might not be anything interesting on the tape, and it's an old machine. I've debated all night whether to leave it there among the roots and debris of the wood to collect moss and fungi for years to come, unless someone takes it away, or whether to go back there and risk being observed by those eyes to get it back, in the hope that it's still working after all the bumps it got yesterday, and see what's on the tape.

At least I can talk to Helen about it now. I go downstairs in the same jeans and t-shirt I wore yesterday, scuffed with dirt and not exactly smelling fresh. Finding clean clothes to put on is never much of a priority for me, and there is no space in my head for it today.

Helen screws up her nose at my grass-stained jeans as I enter the kitchen, seeking breakfast. I busy myself with a bowl and cereal packet, getting milk and splashing it over the cereal up to the perfect level on the bowl (there is an exact art to getting the optimum amount of milk in your cereal bowl), and then flicking sugar over.

I enjoy these small rituals; they calm my mind. I take my breakfast over to the table where Helen sits with her hands around a big mug of coffee. She smiles when I catch her eye but that tightness is there in her expression that tells me she's not as relaxed as she's trying to appear. Bob is still in bed, having a rare lie in after all his hard work in the garden yesterday.

I chew in silence, unsure what to say now that it's all been said. It's like half my weight has been lifted away since our chat yesterday.

'Did you tell Bob?'

'No. He would only worry.' She winks at me, a courageous gesture in the face of Bob's increasing confusion in every day life. The last thing he needs is to be told about ghosts and local legends coming to life when he can barely remember what day it is lately. Helen and I are both worried. Over the last few weeks he's got worse. I had to butter his toast for him the other morning; I found him scraping the bread knife across the kitchen table while his toast went cold in the toaster. He's always been a reticent type anyway, preferring to mind his own business. He wouldn't be able to handle the strangeness of these happenings. In this instant I feel such a surge of love for my granddad, it's all I can do not to run upstairs and give him a big hug as he lays in his bed, trying to sleep. We're losing him, by increments. But as long as he has his vegetables to grow and his paper to look at, he is happy enough. It would not be a good idea to trouble him with anything more complex.

'Do you think he's ever seen anything like we have?'

'Yes, he has. But we don't talk about it. Do you think I should tell him, Tom?'

'It's up to you I suppose. I wouldn't, though. He's happy as he is. Let's let him be happy and not worried.' Helen looks at me with wet eyes, a frail smile on her lips.

I find a grin for her, 'Now I've told you, I don't feel like it matters who knows and who doesn't. We both know, that's what matters to me.'

She glows at that, giving my shoulder a squeeze across the table.

'I'm really glad you told me, Tom, thank you. That can't have been easy.'

'It's okay. I think it's okay.' I'm thinking of my camera, hopefully still exactly where I dropped it, where it landed hard against the unyielding ground of the wood.

'I'm not sure what to do about my camera. I left it in the woods yesterday.'

'Go and get it then.'

'But...' The panic begins in my chest and Helen lays a warm hand on my arm to halt it.

'She won't do anything. Just go in, get your camera, and come straight back out again.' She's pointing with her other hand, indicating what I need to do. 'You have to go to her. She doesn't come to you. If you stay the right side of that ridge, you'll be fine. Might be an idea to not look in that direction, too. Pretend you know nothing about her. You're out getting your camera back, that's all.'

Helen's eyebrows are raised, tense, but not, I think, because of what I'm about to do. It's more a general concern about my habit of making things so cavernous in my mind that I have these panic attacks.

But there's something she's not saying. The Hag has powers. That is one thing all the stories agree on, even Grandma's relatively tame version. Whoever she is, there is something about that pair of eyes I saw for a heartbeat in the wood yesterday that made me want to be certain I didn't put one foot closer, at all costs. I don't need to be warned not to go near. I have no intention of getting any nearer than I have to to get my camera back.

'Do you think there'll be anything on the tape?'

'I don't know, Tom. Best way is to get the camera and find out for yourself.' Helen takes her hand away, leaving a cold spot on my arm where it was. I miss its warmth and the care from it that flowed through to my skin. She gets up and gathers the crockery in the familiar post-meal routine, shovelling it into the sink, pouring hot water, the vapour rising to the window and clinging there like the winter mists in the woods.

Chapter Seventeen

By the time I'm back upstairs I'm certain of what I have to do. There can be no question of leaving the camera where it is and forever not knowing what is or is not on that tape. It was only my fear that made me ever consider that an option. I have to go and get it. No-one else can do it. It has to be me. It's my camera, and I dropped it. But before I do that, there is something else to attend to.

I ready myself and then head back downstairs to ask Grandma if it's okay to go out. I am going to the woods to get the camera, but there is one more thing I want to do first. Someone else I want to talk to. Helen understands how important all this is to me, and says I'm free to use the telephone as much as I need to. I ring Claire's house. She also put her phone number on the letter she sent, not being someone who was shy about doing such things. She wanted to appear open to communication in whatever form I chose, so here I am, making a phone call. I never do that. Claire is still in bed and her father, who does not sound pleased to hear from me, has to go and get her. I hear muffled voices, feet moving over carpet, a distant dog barking. Claire comes to the phone.

'Hi, Tom.'

'Hi, Claire. Sorry I thought you'd be up. Are you okay?'

'Feeling better today, yes, thank you. I thought I was going to sleep forever. I might have done if you hadn't called.'

I pause. 'Any dreams?'

'None!' the relief is clear in her voice.

'Wow.'

A moment's awkward silence while I work my mind around to the point of the call. Claire doesn't bother filling the gap with any of her talkativeness. Maybe she's too sleepy for that.

I take a deep breath, 'I wondered if you might be able to let me have your Auntie Sue's phone number.'

Another pause. I can hear a scratching sound, like

she's doodling on a pad.

'Oh!' She sounds like I've woken her up. 'What do you want that for?'

I hate how wheedling my voice sounds. 'You know we said yesterday we should contact her to see how she is? I wanted to do that, really.'

'Well, I can do that. She's my Auntie.' She says this, but her voice is disinterested.

'Yes, er, I just wanted to speak to her really, about everything that's happened. I'm going to get my camera back today.'

'Why, where is your camera?' I forgot that Claire doesn't know I dropped my camera yesterday. I'm not making a very good job of this conversation. Claire must be imagining that Mrs Roberts somehow has something to do with my missing camera. I have a sinking feeling in my intestines about the next phone call I will make. This one to Claire is meant to be the easy one.

'Sorry, I dropped it yesterday in the wood while I was helping you get home. It's still there. In the wood. So, I'm going to go back and get it.' I cringe, standing in the hallway with the telephone receiver in my hand, wishing I'd gone straight out to get the camera and not bothered with any phone calls.

'Oh. So, what's Auntie Sue got to do with it?'

'Nothing. I just wanted to speak to her, and you're the only person I know who's got her number. And I'm going to get my camera today. I just wanted to speak to her before I went.'

'Oh.'

'I just thought of it and thought, well, no time like the present!' Oh god.

'Right,' she is unconvinced, and I'm not surprised. 'It's upstairs. I won't be a minute.' I hear more shushing of feet on carpet, a door creak and then shut, and a few seconds later the same door open, creak and close. A crackle on the line as Claire picks up the receiver, and speaks much more quietly this time. She doesn't want her parents to hear her giving Auntie Sue's phone number out.

I scribble the number on my hand, not having had the presence of mind to make sure I had some paper handy before calling. Thank goodness there's a pen. I thank Claire, and check once more that she's okay, say goodbye and hang up.

I let out a big breath and release my shoulders, which I didn't notice were getting more hunched and closer to my ears the longer the conversation went on. Keeping my hand on the receiver as it sits in the cradle, I look at the number and run through the possible ways the next call will go. In the end I say under my breath, 'Oh sod it, just do it,' and dial the number.

Sue is not in, or is not answering. I have an inexplicable urge to speak to her before going to the woods. I go through to the kitchen to find Helen is back at the table, having finished that bit of washing up already, and made herself a cup of tea.

I scrape a chair back and sit opposite her, sighing heavily. She starts to chuckle, then checks herself. I must look a fright, making such a big deal out of a little phone call. Neither of us say anything, and after a few minutes, I get up and go back to the phone. I try Sue's number, but there is still no response.

I stomp upstairs and plonk myself onto the bed. Then I get up, put a record on, get my homework out, and slump down on the mattress, making the springs bounce. Five minutes later, I've abandoned the homework untouched and am back in the hall, dialling

Sue's number. There is a redial button but I don't trust it. I always dial again myself. It rings and rings and I'm about to hang up when there is a faint clattering at the other end of the line and Sue's voice, sounding infinitely far away, says, 'Hello?'

I clear my throat, and take another deep breath, 'Hello, Sue? It's Tom. Tom Gibson. From school. Sorry to disturb you.'

'Oh Tom! It's nice to hear from you dear.' She sounds vague, as though only pretending to recognise me and already trying to think of a way to get rid of me.

'I thought I should call you to see how you are, Mrs Roberts. It's been a long time since we spoke, and, well, lots has happened, and... anyway. I just wondered how you were.'

'Oh.' Nothing more.

There is silence on the line. I must prepare what I'm going to say better when I make phone calls. Maybe she's forgotten about me and wandered off on some errand. The silence continues for an uncomfortable length of time. I clear my throat again, my mind empty of words.

'Sorry.' She sounds even further away. 'I think we

should probably not talk about that. Or anything. Um...'

I'm keen to get this over with, regretting ringing her. 'Okay, well, I'm sorry. I just thought I'd ring, but I shouldn't have. So, sorry to have bothered you. Bye bye.'

'Yes, bye dear.' Her voice grows fainter - she can't be holding the receiver anywhere near her mouth - and then I'm left listening to the dialling tone as she hangs up.

Irritation creeps up my spine. The inactivity and restlessness is getting to me. I shrug my shoulders in an impatient gesture that also releases the tension there, and dash upstairs. I push the oddness of that conversation down in my mind, trying to focus on what I'm doing instead of whatever might be up with Mrs Roberts.

All this messing about with phone calls has made me desperate to be active, to be outside doing something. Rushing around to get ready, at the last minute I remember to check the mirror and try to do something with my hair before I run downstairs to the kitchen.

'I'm off to get my camera, then,' I say, all breathless, as if it's nothing more worrying than popping round to a friend's house.

'Okay, Tom,' Helen hugs me, squeezing my ribs. She is surprisingly strong. 'It'll be okay.' She releases me and gives my upper arm a gentle squeeze.

'Thanks, Gran. Just got to do it.'

'You have.'

I grab my anorak from a hook in the hall. I haven't paid much attention to what's happening outside the window this morning, and have no idea if I'll need it or not, but it will fold down small enough to fit into the camera bag once I get it back, if I don't need to wear it.

Pondering these details is comforting, but once outside I'm stunned to find the weather is the same as it was yesterday, and many of the days of this summer before that. It should have been obvious. The sun is not yet at its full strength, but the air is heady with the promise of the heat to come later.

I open the front door again and throw the anorak into the hallway, where it lands in a heap by the skirting board, and shut the door on it. Empty handed, I set off, determined to keep up the head of steam I've built up and not lose my nerve, in the direction of the wood.

*

There is a commotion around the streets leading to the Old Wood. I can only hear it to start with, until I turn a corner and see what's causing it. Another obvious thing I had let slip from my mind in the tumble of recent events; the developers have arrived.

There are cordoned off areas on the main road running adjacent to the Old Wood, and a couple of diggers parked up, with workmen milling around eating sandwiches and chatting. A bit early for lunch, I think, as if that's the most pressing concern here. I keep to the opposite side of the road. The side closest to the wood is impassable to pedestrians because of traffic cones and metal barriers blocking the way. There are signs telling us to use the other path. This is such an insolence, I feel like running across the road and kicking them over, shouting 'Use the other path? YOU use the other path!' I don't, of course.

This must be some sort of preliminary meeting, planning their attack on the wood. I stop to watch them. In my few short years on this planet, I've noticed the propensity for these type of workmen to only rarely be witnessed doing any work. The bulk of their day appears to be taken up with standing around and drinking tea. Well, this lot can stand around and drink tea as much as they like, as long as they leave our trees alone.

I'm thinking about whether any of the workmen can see the shadows, before I remember they only show themselves to children of around my age. Maybe if the shadows showed up and these particular grown ups saw them, they might scare them off so that they went to build their poxy little houses somewhere else.

The workmen are a problem, but there is nothing I can do about that. My camera, however, is hopefully still in the woods somewhere, and I can do something about that. I can go and get it back, and see if there is anything interesting on the tape.

I make my feet move, until I get to the corner where I have no choice but to turn right if I'm going to go to the woods. There is a fresh tarmac smell here, metallic and cloying in my nostrils, made worse by the baking sun. They are resurfacing part of the road near the junction; one of those pointless-looking tasks that gangs of workers like this do between tea breaks, and that makes no real impression on the place. I suppose that's the idea: to improve whilst giving the impression that nothing has happened. What a pity they can't do that with the wood too. Look after it, cut back the brambles a bit, maybe put in a duck pond, and then leave it alone.

I cross, stepping around the fresh tarmac so as not to leave a forever footprint in it, and get to the corner beyond which lies the gate to the wood, so familiar and yet so alien.

It's only a five minute walk from the house, but the low wall cordoning the trees off from the civilisation around them emphasises the separateness of the wood from the village. I run my fingers along the top bricks, soap-smooth and punctuated with gritty dips of cement. They have been baking in the sun since it rose above the rooftops this morning, and are now nicely cooked.

I glance behind me one last time, towards where the workers are moving around in a more purposeful manner. A manager must be about. I lift my index and middle fingers towards them, only for a second, and making sure I'm passing behind the half open gate at the same time so they can't possibly see. Flicking them the Vs gives me a simple, childish pleasure. I only wish there was something more potent I could do.

Hands in pockets, remarkably relaxed considering all

that occurred yesterday, I'm in the wood once more. Those once majestic gates stand behind me and I stop to admire the spectacle of the trees, reaching up like the towers of a Cathedral, trying to reach the sun.

I'm relaxed because I think I'm in the clear. The shadows have left me alone for almost a year. Yesterday, when there were so many of them acting together with such violence, I had seen nothing. It is too hot and balmy a day to keep any tension in my shoulders for long. I'm just going to get my camera and take it back home. Simple.

Not so much as a leaf has moved since I was here yesterday. I'm around half-way to the stump already, striding through the familiar terrain of the Old Wood, but more apprehensive as I get closer to the stump.

A sudden small wind picks up around my feet, startling me, so still was the day up to this point. It's a peculiar wind, only rising to around a foot in height, pushing the denim of my jeans against my legs. I raise my eyebrows, looking around, but there is not enough debris on the ground in this particular spot for me to tell if the wind is affecting all of the wood or only the few feet around me.

It moves the laces of my shoes in all directions. It's not only wind, though. I bend to get a better look. It's not natural. It comes out of nowhere, and the idleness of the day, and of the previous few days, has been so absolute that this disturbance is like something artificial. It has no right to be here.

I crouch down, keeping my eyes towards the ground at my feet, watching the blades of grass getting shoved this way and that by the breeze. I put my hands down to steady myself and see that there is not only wind here, but something else. My thoughts return to the shadows.

Chapter Eighteen

In the wind are specks of a dark grey material, so small I don't see them at first. They are like dust, but more solid. Then it comes to me: ashes. That's what they are, or something else doing a good impression.

I stand again, and now I've spotted them I can see the tiny specks of ash (if that's what they are) without having to crouch, swirling around my feet in a miniature whirlwind. It drifts away, spinning like a Dervish between the trees, confirming for me that it isn't a normal, general wind, but one that was only around me, for that couple of minutes.

Those specks don't feel like anything that belongs in the wood, unless someone has been burning something here, but I would be able to smell that. They have no scent. The only whiff in the air here is the heavy green of the leaves, wilting in the sun, and the distant tang of tarmac from the road. The wind has gone somewhere beyond my vision, twisting around to vanish among the trees. I scuff the grass around me with my shoe in case there might be any clue there as to what caused it, but now that it's gone, all is as it was before.

I inhale deeply, yearning for fresher air to take in that isn't so thick and humid. In the Old Wood, especially today, the air is stale, as though it hasn't moved for weeks.

I focus inwards and see what my breathing is doing, trying to head off any drama that might occur, and a mantra starts up in my mind, repeating in a cycle, becoming white noise, a comforting background vibe. I'm getting my camera and then going again. I'm getting my camera and then going again. It sounds like an excuse I might make at school if I was caught in the wrong part of the building at the wrong time. Sorry Sir, I'm just getting my camera and then going again. Okay, son, be quick about it. I'm getting my camera and then going again.

I walk the thin path worn in the grass by the few feet that pass through here. The day grows cooler by increments as I get deeper under the trees and the sun struggles to get through the branches and leaves. This does nothing to relieve the humidity.

I can see the stump and my camera lying where it must have landed yesterday when I dropped it. Both are far in the distance, my camera tiny next to the great hulk of all that remains of the old tree. So far no new oddities to perplex me like that sooty, isolated wind. It might still be around somewhere, might be back later on, or might have gone for good. I put it to the back of my mind, concentrating on the real, the here and now, and my mission to get to the camera so I can get home.

I can't hear the sounds from the street - the density of trees has grown to block all that annoyance out. The acrid smell of the fresh tarmac is gone. This deep in the woods, it's easy to pretend the rest of the world doesn't exist. It's an impressive place to escape to and will be sorely missed, especially now there is so much more to remember it for than it being a lovely lonely place, and a local legend about a Hag who supposedly lives here. Real or not, that story is so much truer now I've had direct experience of some of the eerie things that can happen in this authentic, dislocated place.

The stump and my camera, tiny by comparison,

loom larger as I approach. I can't see the camera bag yet, which I must also have dropped yesterday. I hope it hasn't been blown away by any little gusts like the one that haunted me earlier.

Right then, I feel a small tug from that wind again, but it's so quick and fleeting I convince myself I'm imagining things. It was only the movement of my feet swishing passed each other in the longer grass that grows under the trees in this part of the wood. That is, until another little puff of wind whistles around my ankles, then vanishes. I try to get a look at it this time but it's too quick. I want to see if I can find those tiny ash-like particles in it, or if this time they're not there.

They are such subtle things, dancing around my feet, reminding me of when I'm in bed first thing in the morning on sunny days and I lay watching the dust motes bubbling in the sunlight slanting between the gap in the curtains. But these are darker, and they move faster with the wind.

I'm close enough to the camera to reach down and grab the handle, and I'm in the motion of doing so when something catches my eye, and I look up to see those eyes, glaring unswerving from beyond the ridge, right at me.

I can't take my eyes away, hand stretched out to the camera. I freeze, before forgetting the camera and straightening up to my full height, looking back at the woman who remains motionless beyond the ridge and the old stump. I can see her far more clearly than I did yesterday: the surroundings are calmer, and I'm not panicked by events outside my control. I'm curious to find it's not so scary this time. Not a petrifying vision, as I had thought yesterday. What it is - I'm searching for the right word in my mind as I stand in plain view of whoever it is - is sad. Infinitely sad. They are the saddest eyes I have ever seen, sadder yet than I know my own can get sometimes. Sadder than Helen's when she's thinking about Bob and how confused he gets these days. Sadder than Bob's when he has that lost look, forgetting how to comb his hair. Almost more sad than I can bear.

I move around the stump, never taking my eyes from the parts of the face that I can see; the forehead and top half of the nose, those eyes, and some of the matted, greasy hair. I stand in front of the stump and as I pause, she disappears, dipping down, and I hear a scuffling as though she's scrambling, or slipping, down a steep incline. I rush towards the ridge, getting there in a few long strides, imagining a far steeper drop the other side than the gentle slope that greets me when I get there. The woman is at the bottom of the slope, heaving for breath.

'Are you okay?' I call to her without thinking, my voice cavernous and echoey in this quiet place. As I tend to when unsure of myself, I speak too loudly, and the woman flinches as though I had struck her. She says nothing, glaring at me, turning her body as if she wants to move further away but can't find the strength. Every aspect of her is grey. Her clotted hair, her blurred blue-grey eyes, her clothes, a woollen skirt and jumper topped with a large, warm-looking shawl, her shoes, damp and misshapen. Even her skin has a pale grey hue as though it has not seen the sun for decades.

'Sorry,' I control my voice with effort, 'I just... are you okay?' I'm climbing up over the ridge to the woman. The strength of her gaze is stark in contrast to the frailty of the rest of her, and as I'm clambering over the ridge, carefully picking my way down the other side where the soil is loose, hanging onto a tree branch to balance myself, I notice another feeble wash of that wind curve around me. It seems to come from the woman, curling through the air, carrying more of those tiny ashen particles away. It plays around my feet and then is gone, as I get to the bottom of the ridge and behold for the first time this mystical place, the 'beyond the ridge' and the 'bower' of all the stories.

I stare about as the woman studies me. The pictures in the books, and that evolve in my mind whenever anyone relates the tale, come to life all around me. I look back to where the giant beech tree once grew and see for myself what a fortuitous vantage point the Hag has found for herself. From here you could see the tree, if it were there to see, and all that happens in its branches, with hardly any danger of being discovered yourself, until an unfortunate child happens to glance down in this direction, and then...

She eats children, I remember, spinning my head back to the old woman in case she is faking her meekness and has chosen this moment to lunge at me. She merely stands, in the same attitude she has had all along, her gaze steady and unwavering.

'So,' I start, trying to keep my breathing under

control. She's just an old woman, that's all. The stories are nonsense. My thoughts tumble over each other as I try to work out how to get out of here without angering her. 'Erm, did you hurt yourself?'

'No.' Her voice is like fine sandpaper rubbing on a smooth surface. Dry with disuse, and the sound of it startles me. I had assumed this would be a one-sided conversation, possibly with a person who is not real like the shadows, or a ghost.

'Oh, they're real.'

I narrow my eyes. One long breath in, hold for three seconds, blow it out. 'P-pardon?'

She actually smiles. Only a tiny turning up of the corners of her mouth, that does not get anywhere near her eyes.

'The shadows, child. They are real.'

'But, how... I didn't say anything about the shadows.' I sound like an idiot.

She lowers her head, making her lank hair fall in slick clusters in front of her face. She turns and shambles away from me, gesturing vaguely with her hand that I should follow. I am not at all sure that I want to do that, so stay where I am, balanced awkwardly, stricken with that self-conscious stiffness so familiar from school. She stops and turns to me again, grinning (or grimacing, I'm not sure which) showing her one remaining tooth hanging from a receded gum.

'Don't worry, child, I won't eat you.' She lets out a chuckle as crackly as dry leaves underfoot, and turns, lumbering off to the dark space underneath the roots of a massive oak tree. Her bower.

I make myself move. I'm here now, so it's not likely I'm going to turn and go back home like nothing happened. Go and pick up my camera and walk home, telling Helen, "Yeah, I was chatting with the Hag, but had to get back for dinner, you know how it is." I follow the woman, and the air grows darker. No sun gets through to this corner of the wood.

The bower is like a giant eye socket, the roots of the trees above penetrating the roof like the tendrils of a plucked orb. All is dank and close. The heat of the day gathers around the floor of the land beyond the ridge. The old woman seems immune to the humidity, in her layers of wool, but a sensible part of my brain tells me to be reasonable - old folk do feel the cold more. I follow her at a distance of around five feet, not wishing to get too close despite how painfully she is shifting her weight along, meaning that I too have to adopt a snail's pace, hovering on one foot in between steps. I try not to make any more sound than I need to.

Thick glistening mosses cling to the tree trunks and roots. Plants grow here that I haven't noticed in other parts of the wood, attracted by the humidity and the lack of disturbance from feet and winds. There are hostas and ferns, uncurling their delicate fingers in attitudes of beckoning, like the girl I saw buried under the tree with that one hand raised up, enticing me forward.

The ground beneath my feet is scratchy with stones, yet spongy in parts because of the moss and the damp. Above, there are only leaves. If I had not just walked here, getting slowly baked by that strong sun, I could easily believe that outside of this bower there is no weather, or none that matters. I bet the snow doesn't even get in here in the winter, but it remains as it is, like an air pocket in a capsized boat, a safe quarter for this old woman and whatever her activities might be.

There is no evidence that anyone lives here, except for the presence of the woman herself. Nothing but the bower, a kind of shallow natural cave carved out under the trees, maybe by the action of water over many years (I learned about this in Geography, and remember being fascinated that water, so soft and pliable, can have such power).

It has not been altered in any way by man-made tools, or by hands, as far as I can see. There is none of the detritus here that humans collect whenever they settle in a place for any length of time. No cooking equipment, no clothes or blankets, no bed, no food, no litter. Maybe there is an invisible force field around the bower that, for some reason, I've been allowed to first see through and then pass through. An invited guest.

I stop, most of my weight on one foot, ready to run if I need to. The old lady has gone into the bower, hunkering down under the roots and settling on her haunches right there in the damp earth. I'm reluctant to follow. That place is too much like a dead end and my escape is already likely to be tricky with the slippery mosses and the bank I had gone up and down to get into here in the first place. I'm sure it's the only way in and out of the bower, but that doesn't stop me eyeing the trees forming the roof of the cave to see if it might be possible to take a giant leap up there and scramble away across the fields. The old woman merely sits and waits for me to finish my hopeless reckoning of the place, and when I run out of possibilities to observe and wild theories to jump to, I look at her too.

'So,' I say again, trying to sound light-hearted, but she holds a bone-thin finger up to her mouth, hushing me.

I purse my lips, unsure what I'm supposed to do. I sway on the balls of my feet, the leg with my weight on it aching, desperate to move, but I can't.

'Come,' the old woman says in her raspy, hoarse voice. It sounds like it's painful for her to speak, although she gives no hint of this on her face.

I hesitate, but relent and follow the old woman's footsteps into the cave, which is every bit as drippy and unpleasant as I anticipated. I wish I had brought that anorak after all so I could spread it on the ground to sit on. As it is, I'm going to get soggy jeans. I lower myself to sit about three feet from the old woman, the moisture instantly working on the denim of my trousers and soaking through to my underpants. I squirm, trying to find the optimum position for minimal dampness on my legs. I settle, and wait to see what happens next.

*

The old woman has stopped looking at me, instead gazing out towards the wood where the giant beech tree used to be. Following her gaze, I'm once again struck by what a great vantage point this is for anyone who wants to see, but not be seen. A perfect spot for a sniper.

'You remember it?' the old woman says.

'The giant beech? No. Sorry.'

She wrinkles her nose, creating more folds of skin in her saggy face. 'The children love it.'

My neck freezes, not letting me turn away from her face. It's a familiar sensation. Whenever I'm suddenly aware of the scrutiny of another person, especially in situations where there are lots of observers (like the classroom, for instance), I get this tension in my neck that won't let me move my head, as the hated flush spreads across my face, with nothing I can do about it. It's happening now.

'Mmm,' I mumble, trying to relax my neck muscles. I give two quick nods, hoping that the old woman doesn't notice, in an effort to free the grip of those muscles which are so against me, and turn to look out of the bower, to the empty space once occupied by the beech.

'I'm a child,' I say, idiotically, as if she might not have noticed. She doesn't glare at me as I expect her to, but that tiny smile reappears on her lips.

And then, out of nowhere, thoughts of Helen come into my mind. The thought of her translates to my lungs and my breathing quickens. I look down to where my legs are crossed on the dank earth and gulp, trying to get it under control. The old woman turns and looks at me curiously.

'Just take a deep breath,' she croaks, 'It's all right.'

I look up, holding the breath in, eyes wide, and let it out, trying my best to keep it steady, not letting my eyes leave hers. I follow this with a few more deep breaths, watching the Hag all the time, studying her face as my breathing calms and becomes more natural. I let her face before me fill my entire vision, unfocusing my eyes like I do with the Christmas tree lights, so that she becomes a grey smudge against the reflective brown background of the damp tree roots. I shove all thoughts of Helen and Bob (who will be furious when he finds out where I am) aside. Two more deep breaths and I let my eyes come back into focus, watching the woman's face emerge from the fog. I'm still here. It's not a dream.

'So,' It is the old woman who says that word this time. 'What have to come here for, child?'

She must know exactly why I'm here. She was watching yesterday when all that happened with Claire and the shadows. She must have seen me drop my camera, just as she saw me reaching for it today when I noticed her.

I can't think what she wants me to say, so I keep quiet, studying her. In any other context, she would not be half as scary. It is the association with the woods, and the stories, that makes her so. And this dark and fearsome cave. I try to picture her sitting in a café having a cup of tea, or tending to a cottage garden, having had a hot bath and change of clothes. I picture her hobbling along a pavement with a Zimmer frame, bumping into a friend and chatting. In that moment, she is simply an old woman, like all the other anonymous old women of the village. They seem to become invisible, all the old women - they fade to grey and vanish without anybody noticing. In this instant, she is one of those. The only difference is that she has chosen to live here, and always wear the same clothes, and never wash.

Despite all the comforting notions I conjure up for myself, there is something about the woman that is unnerving. It's not that she is so ancient, although in truth she appears older than any person has a right to be. It's not the clothes or the neglect of herself, the stench of her unwashed body, or the setting. She has a secret in her eyes. I realise now that must be the key to the reason for her being in this place. I think of the body Claire and I and Mrs Roberts saw out there by the giant beech stump, and the waves of red hair that were revealed to me in my dream. The tip of the nose breaking the surface of those banks of fallen leaves that would never fall again.

I have not forgotten her question, but I'm in no hurry to reply. She already knows the answer.

'I came to get my camera back.'

'Hmmm. Yes, I saw that, boy, but your camera is not here. It's up there.' That bony finger points to beyond the ridge where the stump is. There is no sign of it from down here in the dark and the damp. She has me there. My camera is not anywhere near this hollow place - it's up there in the dry grass and soil.

'Are you the Hag in the Woods?' I blurt out, unable to stop myself.

She makes that crackling sound again, like a small cheese grater is lodged in her throat. Her mouth gapes in a grin that shows her lone tooth, as grey as the rest of her. Her shoulders shudder and her bones rattle. Shaking her head, she settles into her habitual sullen countenance, hiding that rotten tooth from view.

'Well...' She's tracing a wiggled line in the damp soil in front of her with the long nail of her left little finger. I didn't notice it before, but that nail is three times the length of any of the others on her hands. '...I think some people call me that.'

I shut my eyes, willing myself somewhere else. Anywhere. I open my eyes to find her looking down at the doodle she's scratching into the cave floor. I take the chance to scrutinise her appearance. Her hair like boot laces hanging from her head, and the deep folds in her skin. That nail, corrugated from growing too long. The frail, bent form of her, appearing brittle yet supple. I breathe, controlling it.

She glances up, seeing the look on my face, and

laughs again, her eyes scrunching up until I can no longer see them. An eyeless mask of horror and mirth. I try to compose my features, which is hard because I'm not sure what they're doing that she thinks is so funny. Relax your jaw. Breathe. Her face drops soon enough and goes back to her dirt drawing, which is growing into what could be hair. She creates dots and dashes in the soil and an abstract face emerges. The hair could be anybody's; Claire's or any of the girls at school with long, wavy hair. There seem an infinite number of them on days when I'm overwhelmed with hormonal activity and life in general. The face is indistinct enough to be taken for many different people.

'My daughter.' The old woman sighs, her drawing hand hanging over the top of her knee, the portrait finished. That long nail is caked with dirt.

'Your daughter?' I'm lost. This conversation is not taking a course that is familiar to me. I'm useless at conversations. I only hope she doesn't eat me.

The Hag looks up sharply, moving far more swiftly than I thought she was able to. Maybe she does have the strength to drag children to her lair, after all. Her face is morose, scowling, mouth turned down. A rush of cold air makes goosebumps spring up on my skin. I freeze.

This might be the petrifying glare. The one that turns whomever it is bestowed upon to stone so they cannot move or escape. I wiggle my fingers resting on my knee as an experiment. It hasn't worked on me, but it's easy to see how it could work on a scared younger child, caught unawares, perhaps long ago when the old woman had greater powers.

My mind is running away with me. I drag myself back to the present, in a cave with an old woman who is doing nothing more than giving me a horrid, stern look. I spread my hands on the soil either side of me; I am not so repulsed by the dampness now. It crumbles wetly, clinging to my skin. I'm going home soaked through, and there's nothing to be done about it. If I go home.

The old woman's face softens, the creases around her eyes less severe, the eyebrows reverting to their natural position, relaxing the frown. So quietly that I find it necessary to lean forward and cock my head to hear her, she whispers, 'No, child, I'm not going to eat you.'

A blackbird streaks past the entrance to the bower, clattering out its alarm call to the other birds in the trees. The cacophony makes me jump, and sets my heart off pitter-pattering. It's like a shot of reality injected into the dream-like ambience of the bower; a bright, fleeting rainbow across the darkness. After it's gone, the gloom closes around the path it flew until no sign remains that it was ever there.

'They call you the Hag in the Woods.' I'm more reminding myself than giving her any new information.

'I know they do, child,' she returns, her voice back to its gravelly rasp. I sense a great story inside her lifting to the surface. I must be patient and remain here to hear it, even if that means sitting in this damp hollow for hours. The crone sits immobile. I suspect she's adopted this position for untold hours over the years. She's bound to tell me how many years, if I can stay calm and patient enough to hear it.

The sun has moved around and a tiny sliver glints through the leaves, piercing the darkness of the cavern like the narrow beam from a torch. It illuminates a spot of ground outside the bower until the sun moves further around, too soon, and it's gone again. While it's there I notice what look like the dust motes in my room dancing in the thin light, but they are darker fragments of something; those sooty particles. The small wind bearing them has returned. Perhaps it's been here all the time and I've been so focused on everything else that it's slipped past without me noticing it.

I return my gaze to the old woman sitting on her haunches, comfortable, not fidgeting about like I am, and see the particles all around her, coming from her and pirouetting away like the corps de ballet in Swan Lake vanishing into the wings. They behave differently around her than they do around me. I'm an obstacle for them to get around, but they emanate from the old woman. They are of her.

I see that she is disappearing, waning as if a shade is coming across her, painstaking, creeping along her skin. It would be unnoticeable unless you spent a good long while in her company, like I am. In the space of the past half hour or so, she has become less. She is made of paler greys, her outline blurring, her essence withdrawing.

'You're vanishing.' My voice is low.

'Yes.' She sucks on her gums, contemplating, looking far away somewhere past the bower and into the trees of the Old Wood.

'How long have you been here?' My questions feel impertinent, but I'm too curious about her not to ask.

'I don't know.' And then, with infinite patience, she spins her words into a yarn, her arms drifting in and out, the bellows breathing life into her story, which has remained untold for so long. The movement sends the fetid odour of her body to my nostrils. She draws her long fingernail along the lines of the portrait in the earth.

'Your daughter?' I ask, but she shushes me loudly, spittle landing on my forearm. I swipe at it with my other hand, and clamp my mouth shut. Now is her turn to speak. She lifts her arm and snaps it down onto her leg, once again moving faster than she looks capable of. Swirling dust comes from her hand and leg where they impact, and sidles along her skin like smoke.

She calms, absorbing herself in the drawing on the cave floor, tracing the lines over and over, gouging them deeper and deeper, collecting more dirt in that fingernail. Her gaze drifts between the drawing and the space in the air where the branches of the great beech tree used to be.

Chapter Nineteen

'After you had gone yesterday, I remained. I never leave. I was still here in the evening, watching the shadows. Oh, how they make my bones ache. The wood was silent. Those damned bags caught in the trees were quiet. No wind.

'All the shadows dispersed, but it took hours. They didn't want to go. They faded, hanging in the air where they were when you kids were here earlier on. Tendrils drifted away and evaporated to the branches overhead.

'It took such a long time. That one giant shadow. That man. He went last, becoming grainy in the twilight and vanishing, becoming air.' The old woman sucks her gums, her lips squeaking around that lone tooth. I contemplate last night, when I was at home having dinner, and Claire was at her house, tucked in by her mother, being fussed over. The Hag was here watching the shadows, waiting for them to leave. I say nothing.

'It's cold here, and damp. I am not happy. I have been here too long. Sometimes I forget why I am here. I forget all that happened all those years ago, until I happen to look over and see the emptiness in the sky where that powerful tree used to be. Then I remember. Where is he? Where is he?' Her gaze flits to me, but I don't think she expects an answer.

'I know he was here. I've always known it. I feel it vibrating in my bones. It's under my skin. It shimmers in my veins. Yes, they still shimmer, after all this time. I feel it coming up through this damp, cold earth into my feet, and my hands when I fall forwards and land there on all fours like an animal. I feel it through all of me, until it sings out of the tips of my hair, back out into the wood. It goes round and round all the time. I have been here so long. I can't remember how long. It doesn't matter because I was waiting, and I couldn't leave until the wait was over.

'I remember being taller and straighter. I remember washing and caring what I looked like. There was a time when that happened. I had a looking glass, and I used to scrutinise and think about what I looked like. I haven't thought about that in all the time I can remember being here. It doesn't matter. I have to wait. Once the wait is over I can leave, do you see? But not before.' She is far away, those pale eyes roaming over the branches of the trees overhead. I shift my leg to get more comfortable.

'I probably look like I used to, except shrunken. Shrivelled like a prune, is that right? I don't know how that happens. I weakened somewhere along the track. I got lost. But I came to exactly the place I needed to be, and here I stay, waiting. I'm good at it. There's nothing else to do.

'It's so cold. I get colder, though the seasons still change, do they? Spring, or summer. I can't remember. I remember the winters, oh yes. The winters are hard. I don't like them. But I can't remember where else I could go to, so I stay here and try to stay warm. There are rabbit skins I made into a blanket.' I turn my head towards the back of the cave but see only darkness. 'They keep the worst of the frost and the ice away from my skin. It's colder than it used to be, and it lasts longer. I don't know if there are still summers, but I don't feel them. The sun can't reach me. I am made of cold. And I wait.'

I want to tell her 'It's summer now, can't you feel it? The heat?' I want to take her out into the woods, to a gap between the branches overhead and let her skin bathe in it.

'The climb was hard, yesterday. Was it yesterday? I should not have tried that again so soon after last time. My knees ache. Everything aches. I can't remember not aching.

'But I couldn't see from down here. Even I think of this as a bower now. Such a romantic term. I'm a fairy tale character.' She smiles but it doesn't reach her eyes, which fall briefly to the sketch of her daughter drawn in the ground. 'There was such commotion with the shadows, I had to see. I had to get higher. I recognised you. You'd been here before. I saw you, standing up on the stump.' Her face darkens and I regret climbing up there for that panning shot of the woods. She was watching the whole time! A drop of sweat trickles between my shoulder blades.

'Yes, I saw you, your hair all curling over the back of your neck. I was lucky you didn't see me that time, I suppose, but you were so busy playing with that funny recording device.' Her face is lighter, but serious. Blinking, she returns her attention to the trees.

'Moving pictures. Nothing moves here, don't you see? Nothing moving to take moving pictures of. But this time there was a girl too, and the shadows were excited. She could bear a passing resemblance to my Alys. They could be the same. I've forgotten such a lot, but not my Alys' face; I'll never forget that. Same long wavy hair, and something about the shape of her face, now I think about it. Yes. The height too, that was the same. Right height, right age. Hmmm. Poor girl. I wish you hadn't seen me.

'I saw you limping away, leaving your little moving picture capturer in the wood. I'm sure the wood doesn't want it. The shadows lingered like vapours trapped under the lid of a pan. The leaves do that; they trap things. No sun here. No light, only the dim moist air. You had the sun in your eyes. It was really bothering you, I could see that. I don't like the sun either, but it never comes in here.

'I have not seen the shadows do this before. Their usual way is to deliver whatever child they have chosen to the stump and then disperse, scatter like pigeons chased by a toddler in the town square. Do toddlers do that? My memory is dim. But this time they stayed. They liked this girl better.'

Her hands move in front of her, floating until she lets them sink to the ground either side of her picture. I can't take my eyes off her hands, the skin so dry and sagging, and that nail. It's like I'm looking at her on my black and white TV at home. She's colourless.

'This village has been here such a long time, child, did you know?' I give a tiny nod and jostle my legs around a bit more, trying to find a position that is less damp and stiff. 'It's been here a lot longer than most people realise, and it wasn't always called Annisthorpe. They named it for me,' she breaks off in a small chuckle. 'Annisthorpe. Has a nice ring to it. They got my name wrong though. I'm not Annis, at least I don't think so... It's so long since I was named I couldn't say for certain, but I think it began with an 'S', my name.

'I do have a sister called Annis, lovely old name, she moved away over the border into Leicestershire. I wonder what became of her.' Her arms continue that ponderous swimming motion as she talks, coming to rest on her knees from time to time, and all the while the eddies of ashy smoke come from her and she grows an atom paler with each breath. I hope she doesn't fade completely before her story is told.

Her eyes drift between the yawning gap in the forest which was previously occupied by the branches of the beech tree, the sketch on the cave floor, her own hands, watching the smoke idly curl around her flesh, and my face. Each time I move, my jeans un-stick from my skin only to re-stick in the new area where my leg rests. It's as if I'm being absorbed by the earth in the bower, like it will soak every part of me until it and I are inseparable. I sit in this wet place under the oak tree, listening to an old woman. I love stories.

'Maybe Sylvia. Yes, something like that,' the Hag is saying. Her head tilts towards the image in the dirt. 'It was a long time ago we lived here. So long ago. Can you comprehend how long I have been here, boy? Too long. But that's ending now.

'It was in a time before this village really existed. It was a collection of dwellings, only a dozen or so, and we all knew each other. We all got along. We had to to survive. They were simple times. You had to find food, and you had to have shelter, and the procurement and maintenance of those two things took up most of your time. Very simple.

'It was not called Annisthorpe, that is the modern name they gave it, after me,' she can't help another smile at that, finding it too amusing that they had named the village after her, and got her name wrong toboot. 'Maybe my sister will visit one day and think they named it for her.' The smile fades. 'The last time I saw my sister was... I don't know. So, so long ago. Funny, I remember her name but not my own. I've become invisible to myself over the years.' A small shake of the head.

'We lived here, Alys and I.' At saying her daughter's name, the old woman draws in a ragged breath, as though it tastes bitter in her mouth. 'It must be now. I must tell it now. I am fading, see?' She holds up a hand close to my face. It is smaller and less solid looking. I think I could put my hand right through it, but I do not try. Another waft of ashy smoke curls up past my nose, odourless.

'You're a good boy. Alys and I were quite happy, we got along. As I said, you had to or you were in trouble. It was not unheard of for fights to break out and for someone to be sent away to try their luck on their own or wander to the next hamlet to see if they would take them in. It was the worst disgrace to be sent away like that, and if the new village discovered your secret they would be likely to throw you out too. Not much chance of survival for those people. So, by and large, we all rubbed along, too busy surviving to get into too much grief with one another.

'The beech was here then. That's how old it was. It was here then, the same as it is now, in a way. Its ghost lives in this place. Can you feel it?' I nod. I'm not sure if I can feel it or not, but am keen to show I'm listening and to not interrupt.

'It was huge. The biggest tree in the hamlet by a long way. You know how beech trees are. Beautiful things with those long arching branches that seem to go on for miles, and in the autumn all those pretty red and orange leaves. Such a joy, that tree was. The children liked to climb it and egg each other on to go higher and higher and climb out along the branches if they dared, like little squirrels. Children never change, even if the world they're born into does.

'The beech was the centre of the village - the focal

point. We gathered there on special occasions, people got married under it, people were buried under it.' She stops, mouth hanging open, realising what she's said. The air between us sizzles, enclosing the spell she's woven with her words.

She lets out a racking sigh that shakes her tiny body, and sags, head tilting forwards to the sketch of Alys, back bent over so far her chin nearly rests on her knees. She rattles in a long breath.

'When she was fourteen years old, my Alys was killed under that tree.' She points out of the bower to the vast empty space in the wood. 'She had gone out. She often did after all the work of the day was done, and we were sitting by the fire enjoying a nice drink and talking, telling stories. She often went out to get some air, and to have a walk around. She liked to be alone. It wasn't a bad thing to her.' The presence of a kindred spirit comes to me across the years. All I wish for most days is to be left alone to my own thoughts.

'She had gone off somewhere. I wasn't worried, she was never gone for long. She said she never went far. There wasn't far to go, unless she was going to follow the track out of the village altogether, but that wouldn't get her very far either, in her day clothes, with no food or light.

'I was pottering about in the house - we lived in these little wooden round houses, very cosy. I was sweeping up and keeping myself occupied. I didn't like being sat about doing nothing, especially with no company. The room was dark, but everything was dark in those days. We were used to it. I only had the fire for light. A lovely ambient light that is, not like these modern electric lights, never did like those things.

'Alys was gone longer than usual but I still didn't think too much about it. She was a good girl, and sensible. She was probably just enjoying her walk.' The crone turns to me, 'I'm glad you're here, boy, to hear me. Otherwise I'd be sat here all chilly, talking to myself.'

'It got to around midnight when I started to wonder what had happened, but I still was not too concerned. It was a small community as I said and everyone knew everyone else's business - a situation which is at the same time lovely and has its drawbacks - and I trusted the people we lived with, having found no reason not to.

'I wrapped myself in this shawl I'm wearing today. It

was a pale blue I think, then, almost new. I made it for myself the winter before and it soon became my favourite. I put it on and lifted the latch on the door, letting myself out. A couple of dogs barked to each other in the dark, and when they quieted all was silent. The people of the village would all be asleep at that time. An owl hooted in the oak behind the house, and I heard the answering 'too-wit' from its mate over in another tree before me.

'I was not sure which way to head, which way she would have been likely to go, but with that pull that the tree held for the people of the village, it was natural that that was the first direction my feet took me in, without me really thinking about it.

'I passed the little hut where the man who did baking for the village kept his stores of grain, and the farriers, and a couple of other small dwellings. All was peaceful, outside and inside. No one stirred much at night time in the village - we all needed our rest for the day ahead. I went further along past the last hut before the clearing that had formed around the giant beech tree, and as I came around the corner and had a clear view of that place, I saw her.' Her lips pull back, sucking around that tooth.

'She was there under the giant beech tree, and I believe I don't need to describe how she was. You've seen it after all. You and that girl with the yellow hair, and that other girl years and years ago. Quite a few children over the years have seen her. She lay there for hundreds and hundreds of years, and occasionally some unfortunate youth would stumble upon her, discover her only to also discover that she was not really there.' I squint. The body I saw was this woman's daughter, killed how many hundreds of years before! I fidget, folding my legs into a better position, attempting to distract myself from uncomfortable thoughts. Of course it's her daughter; that's what this is all about! I hold the sides of my head so that my thoughts will settle down, then let my hands drop to the earth either side of my legs.

'You filmed her on that funny contraption of yours, out there in the wood, I saw you. I was watching the whole time, of course you realise that now. I used to be much better at staying hidden, hardly anybody ever saw me, but the shadows, they... they've never done that before.'

'Claire.'

'Was that your friend's name? Claire with the yellow hair. But I'll come to that. That's the end of the story. We're only at the beginning.'

The blackbird shatters the gloom, flying back the way it came stuttering its alarm call, oblivious to the cave and the two of us sitting in the shadows. One screaming second, like lightning across a black sky, and then silence. The sun must be out there, hanging heavy like a great medallion, threatening to fall with its weight, but there is no sign of it in here. Other blackbirds chitter in response to the first before the thickness gathers around the bower again like a fret coming in from the sea. The old woman is looking out of the entrance. She can't keep her eyes from the yawning gap left by the beech tree for long. They always drift back there, looking at nothing.

I blink. Of course. She's waiting for something. The old woman's head ticks from side to side, as she intones the next part of her story. Perhaps that's the only way she can get the words through her mouth. No animation or inflections in her voice; a monotone, flat and emotionless.

'I went over to where she was lying, and it was clear that she was dead. I crouched down next to her to check for a pulse - yes, we knew about that in those days, that spirit life throbbing in our necks and how it stopped when we died - but there was nothing. She was gone entirely, nothing there except the empty shell of her body, laid out all askew, and the leaves from the beech tree already blowing across her and resting in the fibres of her clothes.' A tiny shake of the head, and the old woman is human again. Her voice returns to normal. She swallows, making a sticky sound in her neck.

'Well, we moved her, of course, and buried her in the ground not far from the tree, where so many other people had been buried too, as was our custom. We didn't leave her out there on the ground, although I can forgive people who have seen her there since for thinking that we did. She was afforded all the same ceremony and respect as any other in the village. But the difference was that not in living memory had anybody died so young and in such a way.

'Others had their doubts, saying she had some sort of fit that took her life, or she tripped and hit her head on the tree trunk, and that was what did for her, but I knew she had been killed. The way she was laid, the way her legs were and that damned waving hand that has haunted me ever since, all through the years, never letting me rest, convinced me there was a struggle of some kind and she was overpowered.

'I was in the minority, however. Most people could not conceive of anybody cold-bloodedly murdering anyone else in the village. If it was murder, they said, it was someone passing through, a traveller on the road who happened upon my Alys, killed her, and then went on his way, never to be seen again. That was convenient for them. She wasn't their daughter. They couldn't stand the thought that it might have been someone living in the village, someone among us, who had done this, for therein lay the possibility that he might do it again, and that was too frightening. But it had already happened to me.

'Well, the years went by, and I could not extract myself from this place. I grew older, all of my neighbours passed away, the village grew in new and terrifying ways. Men came with machines that were so loud and did so much damage I could barely contemplate it. I couldn't watch, and had to cover my ears when they came thundering by. But they left the wood alone - be thankful for small mercies - and I found a place close to the giant beech tree to live. Here we are. I grew older and older. I would not say I was really living, but I was not dying either.'

She fixes her milky eyes upon mine. It's a long moment before I realise she expects me to say something. I blink and glance down at my hands, at the tableau on the floor, anywhere but into those old, piercing eyes. I remain silent.

Quick as a frog's tongue, a pointed, bony finger darts out and jabs me in the ribs. 'Don't you see it?' she admonishes. I look at her, agog. I don't see it. I have the crushing idea that I've been here so long it has grown dark outside and my grandparents will be wondering what has become of me, like this old woman worrying about her Alys. This could be how it happens. Children aren't mesmerised and dragged to the bower, but simply invited in and not allowed to leave until it's too late, too late for any hope to remain in the outside world of their safe return.

Time is different here. If the crone before me is as old as she claims to be, well, that is hundreds of years old. And as I think these things, I can see that she's dying. Flumes of smoky darkness have been coming from her body the whole time she's been talking, diminishing her. The frequency of the emissions is increasing. Soon there will be nothing left of her.

I can't keep my legs from twitching. My constant fidgeting must irritate her. It's difficult to get comfortable in this hole in the ground. The old woman has been sitting in the same position for the last however many hours with no sign that it's anything but comfortable for her. Maybe she doesn't notice physical sensations in the same way that normal people do. Her eyes have not left me, that finger hovering between us, poised for another jab if I don't say something soon.

'I...'

'You don't know what to say. I know, child. I don't expect you to understand. You've only been on this earth a few short years, and in this bower for less than an afternoon.' She calms, relaxing her hand so it joins the other in their old pattern, floating from side to side as if before her she sees a loom on which she is weaving her tale. Her face softens.

'It's all right, boy. Don't take on so. I'm not going to

eat you, I told you that.' No hint of mirth this time. 'Do you still think I eat children? Oh, I've heard about the stories. Aren't they wonderful? Anything to scare the children enough to keep away from the wood. I don't mind the children playing here, not that they do anymore. But when they used to, I didn't mind. I used to watch them. It reminded me of the village how it used to be, so small, only a few of us.

'Children don't change, whatever era or place. They all want the same thing when they see a magnificent tall tree in their midst: to climb it and see how brave and strong they are. It was always so. That is, until recently. They don't want to do that anymore, and I don't know why. I hope it's not because of the stories about me, as entertaining and colourful as they are. That would be awful. A child's natural purpose is to climb trees, surely?' Her eyebrows raise into an inverted V, 'Do children climb trees these days?'

'Y-yes. Some do, I think.'

'Do you?'

'Well, no. I'm more of a sit on a bench with a nice book sort of child.'

She smiles at that, 'You're only here because of the

stories, aren't you?'

'I-I just wanted to get my camera back...'

'No. In the first place, originally. You came here because of the stories, didn't you?'

'Er,' I can't work out what she wants to hear and I'm scared by this sudden interest in my motives. I don't want another jab in the ribs from those twig-like fingers. 'I-I like the stories.'

'Oh, so do I. Aren't they fantastic? Did you hear, I have blue skin and I can grow to the size of a giant?' She chuckles, the sound making the skin around my hairline itch. 'Such power I have! I never knew I had such power... To drag children... Look at me, do I look like I can drag a child all the way from there to here?' That jabbing finger points at the tree-space and then at the floor in front of us. 'Look at me, I can barely get myself around! There's nothing left of me! I've been here so long I've ceased to exist, except to watch and to wait. That is all I do.' Anger sparks in her eyes. 'I never laid a finger on any child in my long, long life!' Her shrewd eyes turn on me, and in that instant she is witchy, all gleaming eyes and ragged skin. I recoil, but soon she shrinks back into the old woman I've been sitting with all afternoon, hunched into herself, shrivelling.

*

A curious thing happens in the silence, held like a balloon between us. Those wisps of dusty smoke keep coming from the old woman, more often and thicker, and something is changing. A wind rushes into the bower, nothing more than a breath, but it snatches at the crone and pushes her back, dislodging her from her haunches, her shawl falling from her shoulders and hanging about her waist, hooked over her forearms. Her fingertips emit continuous laces of grey sparkles.

Her arms raise up, her face a mask of annoyance, and the shawl falls to the floor behind her. Without it she looks even tinier and more frail. The bones of her shoulders jut out into the thin, filth encrusted fabric of her dress as she shrugs them, attempting to compose herself. Eyebrows up, she sucks on her solitary tooth for a long time, watching her hands. I listen to the squelching in her mouth and the metronomic drip of a root behind me somewhere, giving up its dampness to the bower.

She lifts her head, opening and closing her mouth a

few times, as though trying to speak but not finding any words. She flaps her hands and I sense the urgency in her. She must rush to complete her story. She is fading fast.

'We're coming to the shadows. Yes, that's the next part I need to tell you. Yes, yes, I remember now. Don't pay any attention. I've waited for so long, I'm sorry, child. The shadows. Yes.' I hope the wind didn't make her lose her mind. She coughs.

'It was years after Alys that the shadows first appeared. They chilled me. I knew they were something to do with who had killed my daughter, some kind of clue, and their presence sat in my bones making me ache when I tried to sleep.

'There were not many of them to start with, maybe three or four, but over time their numbers increased until they were like what you saw, and that poor girl who was with you. We're coming to that.' She waves a hand, making sure I don't interrupt. 'That has never happened before, and never will again, I suspect. The shadows have gone now, for good. My bones are hollow like a sparrow's. The shadows lived in me for so long I had no recollection of life without them, and now they are leaving, nothing but dust. Thank goodness.

'They got into the habit of bringing children to the woods over the years, always about the same age as my Alys when she died. Boys and girls, it didn't matter. I knew they knew who killed Alys, so we were uneasy companions, the shadows and I. But I had to stay, because one day they might be careless and let me see what they knew.

'They worked on whatever their purpose was, and I waited. I could not rest until I knew who did that to my girl all those years ago. What else should I do? Go elsewhere and carry on living? Impossible. I waited, right here where you are waiting now for me to finish my story so you can get your camera and go home before dark. It is not dark yet, child, settle. There is more to tell.

'The years went by. The shadows were always around. Although I could not always see them, I knew they were there, somewhere in the village. They brought children and they showed Alys to them, lying there under her drift of leaves, only small bits of her showing.

'She was under the tree, of course she was, that was

where we buried her poor bones, but she appeared to the children just as I had found her, only with more leaves over her. Must have been a ghost, I suppose,' the old woman shrugs, disturbing more of the shadow dust which tumbles from her frame and dips around me on its way out of the bower. A corner of her shawl on the ground is lifted by another sigh of that peculiar wind, and my hand reaches out before I've had the thought that I want to touch it, to see if it's real. I rub the edge of the fabric between my thumb and forefinger, like those frail clippings Mrs Roberts gave me. It's real. I'm satisfied, and return my hand to rest on the clammy ground. She watches me, making no comment.

'The shadows...'

'Yes, we're getting to that now. That part. You came here again with that girl. Sorry, what was her name?'

'Claire.'

'Yes, Claire. Yes. You came here again with Claire. I don't know why of course, that's for your head to keep.' She taps the side of her head with a bent finger.

'There was something about Claire that got the shadows more agitated than they usually were with the children they brought. So restless it felt like scratching under my skin. They were more determined, purposeful. Yes, they really liked your Claire. I told you I always felt that the shadows held the key to my finally discovering what happened to my Alys so long ago? Poor Alys, out for a walk and, well, I don't need to tell you they almost did the same to your Claire. I am sorry for that.'

'She's okay.'

'Is she? She's okay? That is a relief. I was worried about her.'

'She fainted, only for a minute. She got home straight away. She's fine.'

She relaxes at the news, sagging further into herself, a gaping smile on her lips. Nothing more than an ordinary old woman who worries about the kids. She's not some witch or mythological creature, an ogre who wants to rid the earth of children. She is just an old woman who was aggrieved hundreds of years ago and has been waiting for an answer so that she too can rest. She has outlived all of her neighbours and friends, and several generations after them, living here in the shadows, not much more than a shadow herself, and after a time with the shadows inhabiting her poor meek body. I experience such a wave of compassion for the old woman, I worry I might do something rash and hug her, but I remain motionless.

'I'm sorry.'

'It's all right, child. You are unusually perceptive, for one so young. I've lived a long time, too long, and can't remember anyone feeling sorry for me before.

'Nobody knew I was here, except for the occasional glimpse from a child which was apparently so terrifying that this whole mythology sprang up about me. But, you see, all I am is an old, grieving mother who needs to find out who killed her daughter. That's all there is. And where else should I be to find that out but in the very place where my dear girl perished? Once the shadows moved in, I had no choice but to stay and to wait, for I knew they would eventually deliver up the answer to me. And they did.'

Her pale eyes grow moist and I worry she's going to cry and I'll have to comfort her. Despite all my perceptive ability, I'm above all just an awkward teenage boy and the thought of a female crying with no-one else there to take over the comforting duties makes me queasy. She doesn't cry, only looks infinitely sad, as though she has never experienced any other emotion.

'Yesterday... was it yesterday? Yes, yesterday, the shadows were excited. I knew something different was happening. I can't see what was special about Claire. I mean, I'm sure she's a lovely girl, but to me she was just another child brought by the shadows to be shown the macabre spectacle of my daughter lying under the leaves, and there was nothing to mark her out from the other half a dozen or so children who had been brought here before. There are a few physical similarities, but lots of differences too. There must have been something in her spirit that was the same, I think, and that was what attracted the shadows. I'm glad she's all right. But what the shadows did... Could you see them?'

'Not this time, no. Claire was trying to describe to me what they were doing, but it all got a bit confusing.'

'Yes, it would do.' She sucks on her tooth, contemplating. 'I'll tell you what the shadows did this time that was different from all the other times. After showing my Alys to Claire, they rose up tall into one solid form, and that form was a man. I recognised him. It was Andrew Marsden from the village. I mean the village when I lived in it with Alys, the old village, and

I knew then without a doubt it was him who killed her.

'He was unmistakeable, even as a shadow form, even without features. The shape of him, that bulk, and the way he moved - it could be no-one else. He must have died such a long time ago. He must have died way back when I should have. And there he was, all shadow and muscle, pushing that poor girl around. He had pushed my poor girl around, and she had not survived so easily, our Alys.

'I have waited so long to see who... who it was who did that to her. I couldn't leave. I couldn't die, but had to endure here in this damp, miserable place. Because nobody knew who it was, nobody knew who did it, and after a while, so long ago, they stopped bothering to try and find out. It was a lost cause, they said. Was that the phrase? Lost cause. Not to me, she was my daughter. What else should I do? She was so young, what else should I do but remain here, a ghost or a wraith or a real person or whatever I am. What else should I do but wait?

'But now I have seen, and it was him. I never suspected him, any more than I suspected other men in the village. It was such a tiny village, most people thought the man who did it had been someone passing through. A traveller. The thought that it was someone here, who lived among us in this small place where everyone knew each other, where we all lived together as one family, having no choice but to trust and share our happinesses and our griefs around like cakes at a party, was too much for most people, and for me. It couldn't be anyone here. It couldn't be John or Peter or Seth or any of the other people I spoke to every day in the course of procuring food and staying alive.

'But it was, it turned out. It was Andrew. Andrew who worked in the stables, helping the farrier and breaking in the horses. Andrew who brought us all beer in the winter to warm us. Andrew with the big muscles and the scratchy stubble of black hair on his head. The one with the open, friendly face. That Andrew.

'I knew it, cold as those shadows lodging in my bones which made me ache so much I cried. I knew it. The farrier's help from the village. And knowing set me free. I don't have to know why, although thinking about that has kept me occupied for more years than I can count. Perhaps she refused his advances. Perhaps she knew something he did not want getting out. Perhaps he lost his mind.

'So, something about Claire made the shadows reveal the answer to me. And for that I must thank you.' Her eyes are moist, but the ghost of a smile lightens them. 'I must thank you, and when you see Claire you must thank her too, and say I'm sorry if she suffered. It was not me, it was the shadows. They were answering my question. And now it's answered, I don't need to stay any longer. I can go.' The smile stretches across her face, creating yet more wrinkles in her saggy skin.

'What's your name, child?'

'It's Tom.' I try to smile, but am weak, wrung out.

'Well, Tom, thank you for listening to an old woman ramble on. I'm fading, Tom, now that I know. Alys has gone. My daughter, just a girl, who lay there for me for all those years, under those ghost leaves. She was always with me, but now she's gone. Always waving, saying goodbye. She knew all along, but couldn't tell me, and now at last I know too and my skin is getting thinner, I can feel it. There will be nothing left soon. My eyes are drying. I must go. I must go. My story is told.'

Chapter Twenty

The Hag's eyes fade as the story reaches its final phase and she is absorbed into it, a character instead of a real, solid person sitting before me. She is far away. The shadows depart swiftly after her voice ceases, whipping from her wrists and her ankles, eddying around the bower, going for one last look around before leaving for good.

I sit motionless, stunned. The shadow particles enlarge, having no more need to shelter themselves from the eyes of onlookers, trailing away from her fingertips and the ends of her hair, mucky ribbons streaming out of the cave. It no longer matters if they are seen or not, as they will be gone from this world in a matter of minutes.

The old woman lays herself down on the ground of this awful hole that has been her home for so long, and no longer resists the pull of the ashy ghosts leaving her.

There is nothing left to say, nothing left to do. After all these years, there is nothing left but silence, stopped moment by moment by the gentle sighs that emit from her mouth, open to show that one dreadful tooth hanging like the clanger in a bell. I feel a deep empathy with this astonishing old creature, nothing more than a pitiful wraith laid before me. It's as if I can feel what she must be experiencing: a mixture of relief that it's all over, vindication that she was right all along, and a deep, long, furrow of sadness for any of it having happened at all.

I extricate myself from the damp soil and stand up to look down at her body, the cold of the earth piercing through the soles of my shoes. I've been sitting there for so long that even my young bones ache when I rise.

It's hard to believe it can still be daylight, much less a dazzling bright day in the middle of summer, outside of the cave. She thins and pales by the second, and the shadow particles are all around us, meandering through the cave and out of the entrance, taking their time. They are thick and black, not like the wispy pale grey smoke of earlier, as they take the substance from her. Maybe that was all she was made up of all these years. It's an uncomfortable thought that she and the person who killed her daughter could ever have been made of the same material. Although they were both human once, too.

I never found out her name, after all. All I know is it's not Annis, and the people who named the village after her had made one of those quirky errors that history is littered with, and got her sister's name by mistake.

She is evaporating like a cloud after it has shed all its rain. She has her answer, she has told the truth, and now she is released from the grip of whatever curse or blessing it was that gave her such unnatural long life. The stories spoke of her power to make the wind change, but in the end it was the wind that changed her.

She is barely visible. I can see the ground underneath her through her body, which is no more than smoke, rising up to curl about in the air and escape, vanishing into the atmosphere.

*

When there is nothing left of her, her shawl remains on the ground, as solid as you or I. That, at least, is not a ghost. I reach out to rub the fibres again and feel their matted softness. For half a second, I'm tempted to take the shawl home with me, but I can't. It's not mine. Even if the Hag seemed to like me in the end, that is too much of a liberty to take. It should stay here, as the only sign that the old woman who became so reviled by the people of the village who knew nothing about her, had ever been here. If someone stumbles upon it and decides to move it or throw it away, then fair enough, but I won't be the one to remove it from this place. This is where it belongs, as much as the giant beech tree does.

I turn away from the shawl, dark grey and greasy from years of wear, nestled in the hollow here beyond the ridge, and go back into the light of the woods.

The woods, overhung with branches and leaves blocking out much of the sunlight, are twice as bright as the gloom inside the cave where no light, no weather, no life appeared to enter. I have to shield my eyes until they get accustomed to the glare. I climb the ridge, disturbing the soil and lumps of moss on the roots of the trees, and walk back to the stump, trousers and shoes damp and grainy with dirt.

My camera is off to the side of the tree stump. I pick

it up carefully, cradling it in my arms like an injured animal, running my eyes over it to check for any obvious damage. I find the canvas bag a few feet away, and place the camera into it with as much care and reverence as if I were interring the old woman's body into the ground, something I can't do as there is no body left. She deserves that respect. Everybody does.

The afternoon has taken on a lazy, heavy quality, banishing any hint of freshness the morning may have harboured. I walk out of the woods, camera bag clutched to my chest as always, despite the heat, and round the corner onto the street, leaving the green sunshade, the dense atmosphere and the verdant odour of the wood behind.

The sight of the builders shocks me. I had forgotten about them while I was in that otherworldly place. I'm glad. If I had remembered I might have been tempted to tell the old woman about them, and that would have been too much for her. That wouldn't have been fair. A final insult. I am glad she did not know. I observe the workmen and their machinery with a mixture of outright hatred and a heavy sorrow which has not left me since the bower. Then, lowering my eyes to the pavement and choosing to no longer look at or acknowledge them, I make my way home.

Chapter Twenty-One

I get home just before dinner time. Helen and Bob are in the house, getting some much needed respite from the sun. As soon as I'm through the door, Bob tells me he gave up on the garden by mid-morning: the heat wasn't worth it. 'The cabbages and beans can wilt in the sun, but that doesn't mean I have to as well,' he says with a chuckle.

Helen catches my eye when Bob's not looking. Today's been one of Bob's better days so she hasn't had to work so hard, and I'm thankful for that. I come in, nursing my camera, and they are both standing in the hall waiting for me - must have been watching through the window for my return.

Something has happened that I'm not yet privy to. There is an interest in Bob's expression that has been absent up until now, regarding my escapades in the woods. I think Helen's told him. It must have been difficult keeping it from him all these years, and now it's out in the open between us two it must have been more so. I would have liked to have been there when that happened, but I'm glad anyway.

'How did you get on?' Helen asks.

'Fine, Gran,' I beam at them both, enjoying the attention, but I don't want to say too much yet.

'That sun's been very strong, lad, you should have had a hat.' This is Bob.

'It's okay, I was under the trees most of the time,' I'm trying to get past them to the stairs without pushing. They let me pass, aiming questions at me as I start up the stairs, asking if I found the camera, despite it being here in my arms for them to see. They observe that I've been a long time and want to know if I did any more filming.

I'm so humbled today by what happened in the woods, and by Helen and Bob, who took me in when I was so young and have never shown me anything but kindness, although I haven't always been the easiest person to live with. I can't wait to tell Helen, and Bob too if he wants to listen, about it all. This is one of those things that has to be told, regardless of the reception it might get. Some things are too important and have to be said. If the Hag has proved anything, it was that. I will tell this story, if only to these two, and I'm amazed to have no fear about that.

I call back half-answers to their questions as I get to the top of the stairs. 'I have to check the tape!' I call, rounding onto the landing and shutting my bedroom door behind me.

As I wait for the TV and VCR to warm up, and fumble in the bag getting the camera out, I'm thinking about story telling. I would usually be so preoccupied with what people thought and not making a fool of myself, and worried about stumbling over my words, I would be reluctant to speak at all, never mind tell a story. But now, I see that to communicate with people is paramount. Otherwise no-one will know.

Until today I imagined that other people - normal, not-shy people - possessed some kind of secret power that was denied to me, but I've come away from the wood, having spent so long being granted the company of one so old, with an appreciation of my place in the world. I'm not sure how that happened, but it has.

I have things to say, like everyone else, and I'm going to start saying them. I won't wait until the end of my days like the Hag did, to say what has to be said. Helen had waited decades too, and Mrs Roberts, hanging onto those clippings, never telling a soul. I will say it and move on. Where the Hag had stagnated, staying in the same place for what must have felt like an eternity, I will say the things in my heart and keep moving, every day. I hope this wave of confidence stays with me.

I have to see what is on this tape. The machines are ready, the VCR hums, the TV produces white noise.

I put the tape into the video player and rewind it, tapping my fingers as I wait for it, the whirring growing more frantic until it stops. I press 'play'. I watch the whole thing through, never letting my eyes leave the screen, and keep them there after the tape has finished, the screen black with horizontal scratchy lines skittering across it.

After a while, I blink and look down at the carpet, wiping at my eye with the back of my hand, where a heavy tear is threatening to escape, making my head ache. I wipe my hand on my jeans, shake my head, blinking back more tears, and get up to check my face in the mirror attached to the wardrobe. I hardly recognise myself. What a day. Leaving the tape in the machine on the floor and the camera on the bed, I switch everything off and make my way downstairs.

Helen and Bob are in the living room. The television is not on. They are not reading the paper, or doing a crossword, or knitting, or talking. They're simply waiting. I've had enough of waiting for one day. Not my waiting, there has been hardly any in my short life, but other people's. I stride into the room, taller than before, not hunching my shoulders for once, and sit in the spare armchair facing them both. I clear my throat and can't help smiling at their expectant faces. I'm going to tell them a story. I take a deep breath and relate the events of the day, every detail. I only stumble once or twice, when I get things in the wrong order and have to rewind, but I set the story free.

*

Afterwards, we are all eating a dinner of chicken pie and chips. I'm touched that Grandma has made my favourite and feel that tear threatening, rubbing at my eye to get rid of it. Bob looks at me over a forkful of peas he's trying to get to his mouth without dropping any. As soon as he shifts his attention, a couple roll off onto his plate.

'You did a good thing in the woods today, Tom. I'm proud of you.'

I'm too stunned to speak, thankful for the mouthful of pastry I have which means I have some time to cogitate before any response can be expected. I nod, pointing at my mouth, indicating I'll get back to him as soon as I've finished chewing. After one final, massive gulp, I say, 'Thanks Granddad Bob. I love you.'

Bob's face turns a bright red the beetroots in his vegetable patch would be proud of and beams at me, specks of pea stuck between his teeth. He freezes like that, before remembering his dinner and getting another forkful.

I turn to Helen, 'And you, Helen.'

Helen's smile is immediate and huge. 'You too, son,' she says, and her eyes get moist as she blinks and goes back to eating.

*

I have to wait a while until I can reveal what's on the tape. I think about showing Helen and Bob, but they say they aren't too bothered about seeing it, their curiosity having been slaked by my telling of the events.

The leaves are turning by the time I remove the tape from its hiding place among the socks and underpants in my top drawer, the safest place I could think of for it. It's well padded in there, and it's a drawer I open every day so I can check it's okay.

I have used the camera a few times since the woods, with fresh tapes in it. I'm getting quite good with it, and have notes about films I want to make stacked by my bedside. A week ago I made a short film, documentary style, about Bob and his veg patch, for which Granddad was an enthusiastic participant, talking at length and with great passion about his leeks and potatoes, and how his sprouts have come up this year. That was a good day. He's missed his vocation, Bob has. He should be on a gardening programme on the television or radio. But he's happy with his lot, that much is plain to see.

I'm in my school uniform and setting out for the first day back after the long holiday. It has cooled, and there have been a couple of days of rain in the past week, so it looks like the heat has broken and for that I must be grateful. I pull on my blazer, not needing an outside coat as well. My anorak is scrunched up in my school bag in case of rain later.

The last thing I make sure to take with me today is the tape, extracting it with great care from my sock drawer, wrapping it in some hankies, and placing it in my bag. Even though it's small enough to go in my bag and not be noticed by anyone, I'm not sure about taking it into school. It's precious to me. Hopefully all the bullies will be too preoccupied with a fresh new crop of pupils to size up to bother about what I have or haven't got in my bag. They have taken it from me before, scattering the contents over the whole playing field, seconds before the start of lessons.

It's an age until the bell goes for lunch and I make straight for the big staircase in the main building, once more going against the tide of masses of pupils all going the other way, desperate to be out of the building and across the yard in the hall eating their lunch, or else it's fine enough to hang around in the playing field, eating and talking and half-heartedly kicking a football around at the same time.

The sun beats down through the huge, cathedral-like windows. It has not given up trying to fry me yet, and I sweat inside my blazer. I reach the top, out of breath, the sweat trickling down my sides, and take a second to compose myself outside the library door.

She's sitting where she always does, at her desk halfway along the same wall as the door. She looks up as I enter. We are the only two in the library. Nobody wants to spend their lunch break on the first day back at school in the library: there's too much sunshine outside and too much catching up to do after the long break.

'Oh!' Mrs Roberts says, and falls silent, an uneasy smile tugging at her lips.

I grin openly, 'It's okay.' That seems like the right thing to say.

I cross the room to her, swing my bag down off my shoulder and open it to get the tape out. 'I've got something to show you.'

She says nothing, but peers at the tape in my hand, eyebrows raised. She goes over to a far corner of the library, behind a part of the shelving that juts out into the room for six feet or so, behind which the library's old television resides on its trolley. She wheels it out, far enough so we'll be able to watch it without having to disrupt the rest of the room. I'm fairly confident we won't be disturbed here, in the relatively dingy library on such a glorious sunny day, and the first day back at that. I leave my bag on Mrs Roberts' desk, and amble over to the television, slotting the tape into the video player on the rack underneath it.

Mrs Roberts sits on one of the desks close to the screen. I'm pleased she seems keen to not miss a second of this. I join her. At her touch of the remote control the TV flickers into life, shortly followed by the VCR, and the tape starts.

I've only ever seen this tape on the black and white portable in my room before, and I'm struck by the colours. They are more vivid than I remember them being in the real wood. It's like I'm back there on that hot day, the depth of the colours making the happenings on the screen all the more real. I've seen the tape many times and know exactly what to expect, but I'm as absorbed in it as Mrs Roberts.

'It's nice to see you, Tom.' Mrs Roberts' voice is low over the humming of the tape in the machine.

'You too,' I say.

The film shows the woods, the camera jiggling this way and that with my walking action. Mrs Roberts gasps when Claire appears on the tape, putting her hand to her mouth and looking to me. I nod and incline my head towards the screen to indicate that she should carry on watching.

'She's acting very strangely,' Mrs Roberts whispers. The tape shows Claire stopping and looking all around her, describing what she sees, her voice barely audible on the tape.

'She's seeing the shadows that you and I saw,' I tell her, 'but these are different. Keep watching.'

The film continues as I follow Claire through the woods.

'Going to the beech stump,' Mrs Roberts says, her voice dreamy.

The film shows us meandering through the woods, with Claire all the while looking distracted and talking about what she is seeing until we get close to the stump and then she is silent. The drama unfolds and I glance at Mrs Roberts who is open mouthed. At the moment that Claire falls to the ground, she lets out a louder gasp. 'Oh my gosh, is she all right?' She turns to me, eyes wide.

'Yes, she's fine, she was fully recovered by the next day. This was weeks ago. She fainted, but she's fine.' I find it necessary to take a stride over to the video player and pause the tape while I say this as I don't want her to miss the next part. I press 'play' and take up my position next to Mrs Roberts on the desk.

After the shadows have overcome Claire, and I've tried my hardest to fight them off, flailing against things I can't see and dropping my camera in the attempt, all the tape shows is the ground the camera fell onto, tufts of leaf debris and stubby blades of grass growing from the side of the screen. A couple of times a foot or leg comes into view as Claire and I are getting back up to our feet, and then are gone.

But there in the distance, unmistakable despite the grain of the film and the tilt of the camera, is a pair of pale rheumy eyes set in a face as grey as a rain cloud, marked with lines and creases. An ancient face with lank, greasy hair springing from its head. The face is beyond the ridge, and is the Hag, who has seen the whole thing and is looking directly into the lens, unblinking.

A few seconds later the tape stops and Mrs Roberts turns to me. She has tears in her eyes, but controls herself, gulping them back. I smile, but take that stride again to press 'eject' on the video player and get my tape back, suddenly finding the proximity to Mrs Roberts to be too intimate.

I go over to her desk where my bag is, without saying a word, and take my time wrapping the tape back up in the hankies like a Christmas present, and placing it in my bag. I've shown her, which is what I knew I must do the moment I first saw it for myself, and now I can go.

'Thanks, Tom,' she calls from across the room where she's sitting on that desk, watching me, a big smile on her face. 'Thank you!'

'It's okay,' I return the smile, a little shier than hers, and leave the library.

*

After that, I show the tape to my grandparents too, who's response is similar to Mrs Roberts', though they have more of an idea of what to expect. I keep the tape in my sock drawer for a long time until Bob puts a new shelf up in my room for all the films I'm making, and that particular cassette is wrapped carefully in tissue paper and placed at the end of the shelf near to the adjacent wall, so that it's safe.

I think about showing the tape to Claire many times, but I don't see much of her after that, and the longer I leave it the harder it becomes to bring the subject up when we do meet. To this day, she does not know.

November, 1977

'It's in a lovely area, too!' Mum is sitting at the kitchen table, chair stuck out in the middle of the room. She can't get as close as she used to, and has her back straight, legs apart in her dungarees, reaching over her huge tummy to pick up her coffee cup.

'I think this might be the one, Pam.' Dad is in a brown suit and tie, coming in from the garden where he has been sucking on his pipe. He sometimes takes the pipe into the garden when the weather's nice, so the house doesn't get as smoky. 'We need somewhere a bit bigger now...' he nods towards mum's belly instead of finishing the sentence. She giggles into her cup, making the coffee bubble.

I've got Ready Brek with extra milk. It's fiery going down, that mellow oaty taste. They are deciding whether to take me with them tomorrow when they go to look at the new house. I tell them I'll stay with Grandma.

THE END

Author's Note

The creature, Black Annis, is said to have lived in Leicestershire where she roamed the Dane Hills. She had a blue face, claws of iron and an insatiable hunger for child flesh. When she had eaten the children, she tanned their skins and hung them out to dry before wearing them around her waist.

There are a few theories as to where the legend comes from, but it is generally agreed that she is an English form of the ancient crone goddess, devourer of souls, which features in all mythologies worldwide.

About the Author

Deb Scudder was born and raised in Lincolnshire, England, and is inspired by her memories of growing up there and her love of folklore and fairy tales. The Hag in the Woods is her first novel.

Printed in Great Britain
by Amazon